The Language of Elk

The Language of Elk

Benjamin Percy

Carnegie Mellon University Press
2006

Many stories in this collection have also been published in the following:

Sycamore Review: "Unearthed"

Greensboro Review: "The Iron Moth" and "The Language of Elk"

Rosebud: "Bigfooting"

Hayden's Ferry Review: "Winter's Trappings"

SWINK: "The Bearded Lady Says Goodnight"

Idaho Review: "Swans"

Book and Cover Design: Neal Shyam

Library of Congress Control Number: 2005933839
ISBN-10: 0-88748-454-9
ISBN-13: 978-0-88748-454-4

Printed and Bound in the United States of America

10 9 8 7 6 5 4 3 2 1

CONTENTS

For Lisa

Unearthed

Denis began acting strangely soon after he dug up the dead Indian. This happened in Christmas Valley, in Eastern Oregon, among the sand dunes and sage flats and rimrock canyons where he and his son, Elwood, often spent their weekends. They called themselves rockhounds, fossil hunters, archaeologists, and they carried on their backs shovels and picks and trowels and paintbrushes to whisk away the dust and calcite. When they hiked through the high desert, their eyes studied the soil for the sparkle of a quartzite vein, the scattered depressions of a long-rotted Paiute village, some hint of treasure, some sign they might point to and say, "There!"

They dug up thunder eggs, opals, petrified wood, fist-sized agates that seemed to emit a foggy light, like tiny suns breaking through a cloud. In a grotto with a small spring bubbling from it, they discovered a deer skull encased in rose quartz. And in the Mt. Mazama ash—as hard-packed as kiln-cooked clay—they found fossils of all sorts, of leaves and clams and ferns. After they filled their Bronco and drove the hundred miles back to Redmond, they cleaned their treasures and labeled themand put them on display so that their house resembled a museum.

In the center of their dining room table sat the rose-quartz skull, glowing pink, like a crystallized ham. Their bookcases and tables overflowed with precious stones, and their walls were crowded with velvet-lined display cases holding chirt and obsidian projectile points —"*Not* arrowheads," Denis would say. "Arrowhead is an all-encompassing hack term that should *not* be used with reference to carving tools or spear and atlatal points." He talked like that, like a textbook—using words like prismatic and tetrahedron, occipital, Macedonian—and Elwood listened to him with the same polite disinterest he gave his tenth-grade teachers.

Which was not far off the mark. His father worked as an anthropology lecturer at Central Oregon Community College—though at first glance you would guess him a construction worker or a truck driver, not a scholar. Years ago he had played catcher for the Oregon State Beavers, and he looked like a catcher, at once too short and too wide for most clothes. When he got excited, he would repeatedly pound his hand into his palm as if it were the peach basket of a mitt.

Elwood loved and half-loved many things about him, but more than anything, he felt sorry for him. How else can you feel about a man who randomly bursts into tears—at the grocery store, the movies, the buffet at the Golden Corral—mourning his dead wife? What else can you do except follow him into the desert, where there were no enclosures, where everything seemed to draw a free breath, and where the two of them regularly escaped the present in a quest to dig up the past?

Elwood remembered his mother, Misty. He remembered her hair, a deep brown, almost black. He remembered how she always wore tank tops and how the bones came out of her shoulders like angel wings. He remembered his father constantly telling him how sick she was, how very sick. He remembered the medications—the Prozac, the Lithium, the green-and-white pills meant to tame the yo-yo effect of her bipolar condition—and how they sometimes made her act drunk, made her dizzy, made her slur her words. She would stroke his cheek and look at him with her eyes half-lidded, like a set of collapsing moons, and say, "My Elwood. Thank God for my Elwood." He remembered her laughing one instant, sobbing the next—one time lurching up from the dinner table with sudden tears on her cheeks, sweeping the turkey off its platter, onto the floor, because his father said it tasted, "A bit dry, but good."

And he remembered, finally, the night she shook him awake and said, "You know I love you, right?" Somewhere between waking and dreaming, he saw her hovering above him in the dark and he said, "Yeah, Mom. Love you, too." She left him then and he lay there, still tangled in his dreams' cobwebs, realizing too late—after he tossed away the covers, after he hurried down the hall, down the stairs, after he heard the snap of the rifle—that something was wrong.

She left him a red carnation of brain matter on the wall, and on the kitchen table she left him a letter, its handwriting so sharp and hurried it reminded him of barbed wire. "I'm so sorry," it read. "And I know that doesn't mean anything. I know that's just a bunch of shitty words. But I'm really truly sorry."

It didn't make any sense. *She* didn't make any sense. He tore the letter up and let its pieces flutter into the toilet, but six months later the words remained imprinted on his brain like the patterns of a long-dead leaf, fossilized by the intense pressure of the moment.

Summers in Eastern Oregon, the wind blows in heated gusts, like the breath of a big animal. The July day Elwood and Denis discovered the dead Indian, to keep the seething grit from their eyes and lungs, they wore sunglasses and tied wet bandanas around their faces as bandits would.

They were hiking through a shallow canyon when they noticed among its basalt pillars a six-foot notch with a cool wind blowing from it, indicating depth. This wind brought with it a low drone, like someone blowing across the mouth of an open bottle. They clicked on their flashlights and ducked inside and the notch opened up into a cave over a hundred feet deep and thirty-feet wide.

They took off their sunglasses and bandanas in a hurry. Here, breathing was like drinking from a cellar floor puddle, a taste both cool and mineraly and tinged with mold. Their flashlights spotlighted the many suns and rattlesnakes and antelope and men with gigantic penises that covered the walls. Some were pictographs—colored blends of ocher and blood and berry juices—and some were petroglyphs, crudely chipped into the stone. Above all this hung many bats, chirping softly in their upside-down sleep, their brown bodies tangled together and moving so that the cave seemed a living thing.

"Man," Elwood said, and Denis said, "Wow."

Denis took out some butcher paper and held it against a petroglyph and rubbed it lightly with a crayon. The image of a pig or a bear or a dog—something—transferred onto the paper, and he rolled it up and put it in a plastic tube.

It wasn't long before they prostrated their bodies and began to dig. Their fingers had darkened and thickened from so much time in the desert, and they used them now, along with their trowels, to claw away the soil.

For the next several hours they filled their backpacks with the cave soil—so cool and black with guano—and carried it outside, dumping it in a pile that grew larger as the cave grew deeper. They discovered a seed cache, a thick layer of charcoal, obsidian chips, and a collection of bones, so broken they no longer had names. Then Elwood's trowel scraped across something smooth and brown.

"Dad," he said. "I think I've got something here."

The Indian had been buried upright, in a fetal position. A soft cocoon of dust and papery skin surrounded its brown bones. Elwood and Denis whisked away the soil, revealing first the skull's round crown—erratically haired—and then the hollows of its eyes, and then its shriveled nose, its teeth showing in an eternal snarl.

The more they unearthed, the more agitated Denis became. He pounded his fist into his palm, his cheeks glowing a painful red, his breath coming in big gusts as if some desert storm brewed within him. From the look on his face, Elwood could not tell if his father was blissfully happy or simply afraid.

"Dad?" he said. "You okay?"

Denis ran a hand across his face, leaving dirt there, and said, "Are you kidding? This is unbelievable. I'm in Paleolithic heaven, buddy." Despite his apparent enthusiasm, his voice struck Elwood as robotic, insincere, as a gray thing that swallowed emotion and gave nothing back.

Buried with the Indian were a pipe, a knife, an at-latal, a pair of moccasins, and a decayed leather robe braided with elk teeth. Denis and Elwood took everything.

They never thought about the legality or the *rightness* of what they did. They only knew that it brought them pleasure, somehow—taking these things, these hidden treasures, and making them their own.

It was nearly night when they left and a massive flapping followed them as hundreds of bats escaped the cave, like ashes blown from a chimney, riding the hot gusts into the purpling sky until they were lost from sight.

Their house was an ordinary house—a tan two-story box with plastic siding—except that it was full of dead things. Bones and fossils, tools from long-dead tribes, and now, a mummified Paiute Indian. Denis carried the body across the threshold as you would a bride, proudly, staring down at the thing in his arms as if it held great promise.

He could not decide where he would put the Indian. On the end table in the corner of the living room? Perched on top of the television, the refrigerator? Or how about…Denis removed the rose-quartz deer skull from the dining room table and replaced it with the corpse…how about here?

Elwood watched all this with a vague sense of disgust, and when his father asked him what he thought, he said, “I don’t really like it anywhere. I don’t really want it in the house at all.”

Denis gave him a look, like: why on earth not?

Because of the dresses hanging in your closet, the perfume in the bathroom, the photographs staring at me from the mantle, the spackled section of wall where the bullet lodged itself like a seed. Because this house is full of too much death already, is what Elwood wanted to say, but didn’t.

“It’s a dead body, Dad. It’s creepy.”

“Hmm,” Denis said and looked at the Indian as if for the first time. It sat on the table, its bones shining dully beneath the chandelier, like some spirit summoned by séance. “Maybe you’ve got a point.” He scooped up the Indian—it was quite small, weighing ten, fifteen pounds at most—and sort of rocked it in his arms, peering around, seeking a place for it.

“I tell you what,” he said. “If it bothers you that much, I’ll keep it in my bedroom. Locked up tight. Okay? Don’t you think that’s a good place for it?”

From where he stood, some five feet away, Elwood could smell the Indian. It smelled like mothballs and old fruit. One of its eyes was pinched tightly closed—the overlying skin a greenish black color, like that of a diurnal bird—while the other eye was a gaping black hole. From this Elwood felt he was being watched.

Ten days after Misty died—the middle of February—Denis demanded Elwood come outside and play catch.

"But it's freezing," Elwood said, and Denis said, "So put on a fucking coat." Elwood had never heard his father swear: he did as he was told.

Snow fell when they faced each other across the front lawn, the grass frozen and crunching beneath their feet. They began to lightly toss the ball back and forth, and then their muscles limbered and their aim improved and the speed of the ball increased, until they were hurling it at each other, throwing as hard as they could, as if their lives depended on it. They would seek out the ball with their mitts, zapping it from the air, pocketing its speed, and then—with a full windup, a big windmill motion—they would whip it back in the direction it came from. The snow grew thicker, the air colder, and before long, their hands went numb and they could hardly see the ball as it sizzled through all that whiteness. Cars slowed to watch them, the drivers no doubt smiling at first, and then gasping, saying, "My word," when they realized they were not witnessing a snowball fight but something else entirely.

Then Elwood got struck in the forehead with such force his sinuses bled out his nose and an immediate lump rose between his eyebrows. Denis said, "I'm sorry. Jesus, am I sorry," and carried Elwood inside and cleaned his face with a cold washcloth and helped him to bed and placed an icepack over his eyes.

Since her suicide, they had not talked about Misty, but now they did. There was something about hurting his son that made Denis feel so guilty, he wanted, he *needed* to bring out a hurt of his own. "Elwood?" he said. "You want to hear something terrible?"

Elwood did not. Every sound, every bit of light, seemed to intensify the red throbbing behind his eyes. But he listened, and his father finally said, "I more than once wished she was dead." He laughed quietly, wretchedly. "You know how it is, you get in a fight, you see some beautiful woman on the street, and you think terrible things? You think: *man*, how great would it be if tomorrow the wife died of brain cancer or whatever. You don't really mean it, but you think it." He blew a sigh out his nose. "It's awful, I know."

There followed a long silence, and then Elwood took off the ice pack and locked eyes with his father before reaching out and taking his hand and asking if he, too, felt weighed down by like, say, fifty pounds of grief?

"Yeah," his father said, his eyes stained yellow as if exposed to something toxic. "More like a hundred-forty."

This was the last they spoke of Misty, except to ocasionally say, "Jeez, do I miss her." There was an understanding between them. They had both lost the love of their lives and a bond like that makes words more often than not unnecessary. She was always there, between them, like an awkward silence Denis sought to fill, first with baseball, then boxing, hunting, fishing, Chuck Norris movies, and finally, the desert. Here they would peel away the soil and smash open rocks and loot the dead for as long as it took them to answer the question: What next?

The Monday after they returned from Christmas Valley, Elwood thought he heard voices coming from his parents' room. He peeked inside and saw his father sitting on the edge of his bed, and next to him, like some primordial stuffed animal, the Indian.

Without Misty, the garden had gone wild. Dandelions and crabgrass took over the sod, weeds choked away all the flowers except the sunflowers, and morning glory and kudzu vines groped their way up the house, to the roof, tangling their way across the second-story window Denis stared out of now.

The leafy vines shaded the room, and when the breeze blew, a flashing green and yellow light shuddered across Denis and the Indian, and he stared at the window as if it were a television, his mouth agape.

"Dad?"

Denis snapped shut his mouth and looked at Elwood as if he didn't recognize him. "I didn't hear you," he said in the too-loud voice he sometimes used on the telephone. "You spooked me." He protectively put his arm around the Indian and drew it a little closer to him. Some blackness remained where it had sat before.

"Dad, I thought you taught class on Mondays?"

His forehead creased. "That's correct," he said. "I do." He lifted his arm and examined his wristwatch, and then his arm continued its journey up and he squeezed the bridge of his nose. "Dang."

Sometimes his father looked emotional enough to kiss Elwood on the mouth. Other times—such as right now—his eyes seemed unfocused, his words distant, as if he were someplace else entirely. This had been happening more and more often—until his standard state of mind was elsewhere and nowhere.

Missing the occasional class was par for the course.

No big deal, Elwood thought. Nothing to worry about.

Then Denis began to paint. He bought a crate of salmonberries at the Farmers' Market and with a mortar and pestle he mashed them, filling a big bowl. He added to this blood—brought out of his thumb by a tack—and then carpenter's glue, which thickened the mix into a bright red paste. He applied it to the living room walls with his fingers and with a stick whose end he hammered and chewed into a bristly brush, painting animals and hunters and suns and strange geometric patterns. Above the couch, over the spackled section of wall, he painted a crude rendering of Misty, so red she seemed on fire.

He did all this with the Indian seated on the La-Z-Boy recliner, supervising, and when Elwood came home from baseball practice and saw his father's hands gloved in blood, when he saw the murals swirling around him, he could only say, "Dad?"

Pizza Hut was where Elwood worked part-time over the summer—in the back, since he didn't like dealing with customers. Here, the conveyer-belt oven blasted heat, a heat so tremendous Elwood imagined it as the source of the Eastern Oregon winds. With temperatures hovering around one hundred degrees, he would sweat through his clothes and season pans with cornmeal and flour, garlic and salt, and he would stretch the refrigerated dough balls, at first caressing them—sometimes imagining them into boobs—and then squeezing, kneading, tossing them with an artful flick of his wrist—*up*—fitting each pie perfectly into its pan, and then painting it with sauce and cheese and meats and vegetables.

He liked it. He got lost in the heat and the repetitive motions.

His daze broke when from the front register came a shout: "Elwood! Hey, Elwood!" His manager, Joanne, an overweight grandmother with a cigarette voice, was motioning to him with one hand and to his father with the other.

His father stood across the counter, waving, his face painted with what Elwood recognized as baseball grease. Six black stripes started at his eyes and ended at his hairline like tall eyelashes or backwards tear trails. His chin and cheeks were patterned with swirling designs, the kind a cartoonist would use to indicate wind.

Elwood wiped the sweat off his face with his forearm and went to him. "What are you doing here, Dad?"

"I always come here." Which was true. He often dropped by during Elwood's shift. "Just saying hello."

Elwood noticed some people in the buffet line staring. "But what are you *doing* here…like *that*! Like it's Halloween."

"Pretty cool, huh?" He smiled and touched his face lightly and checked his fingers for paint. "I'll do you later, if you want."

"I don't think so, Dad."

"Okay." They stood there a moment, just looking at each other, and then Denis said, "Hey, I just wanted to let you know I'm going to a bar tonight. I won't be home when you get home."

"You? A bar?" Elwood would not have been more surprised if his father said the world was flat and cows came from outer space.

"I know this may come as a shock to you, Elwood, but I need to have fun. I need to intermingle with people. People of the opposite sex. It's part of the healing process."

"Whatever. I don't care." Which was not entirely true, but Elwood felt more stunned than upset. "But you can't go like *that*. You'll get beat up."

"It's Cowboys and Indians Night down at the Wounded Soldier Tavern. I'm just adhering to dress code." Here he winked, and Elwood noticed the Atlanta Braves shirt, the fringed buckskin pants, and the moccasin bedroom slippers his father wore. "I'll see you later, bucko." With that he patted his mouth with his hand and made a woo-woo noise and rain-danced his way down the aisle and out the door.

Later that night Denis came home with a woman.

From his bed, propped up on his elbow, Elwood heard them laughing in the kitchen and then whispering in the hallway as they tiptoed past him and clicked closed their bedroom door.

There followed a great deal of moaning. Elwood felt simultaneously aroused and disgusted. The bedsprings began to chirp, the headboard began to thud against the wall—and in her final excited release, the woman made these *yee-yee-yee* noises that reminded Elwood of coyotes barking.

His mind was still hazy from sleep when he shuffled downstairs for breakfast and saw his mother in the kitchen, doing dishes, bending her knees and singing quietly, a sort of undersong to the bluegrass playing on the radio.

She was lovely to look at, her dark rolling hair and soft brown eyes.

Hello, Mom—Elwood thought—Did you know I just can't seem to get you out of my head? Everywhere I look *there you are*—at the grocery store where they sell mangoes, your favorite fruit, and in the woods where I see the Columbine you might have stuck in vases. And now you have returned to your kitchen, miraculously reincarnated, making me think that night with the rifle was nothing more than an elaborate joke, a dummy covered in ketchup.

One year later and here is the punchline: Dad and I can't get along without you.

His mother turned to grab a dishcloth. When she turned she turned into an Indian woman who dried a coffee cup. Last night flashed through his mind—he could hardly believe what had happened *happened*—and she blew on a dirty spot, her lips pursing into kissable goodness, and Elwood wished more than anything he were that cup.

She noticed him standing there and clicked off the radio. "Morning," she said, and he said, "Hi."

Her hair was long and black and her face was round and brown. She was pretty, Elwood thought, but a different sort of pretty. Not as pretty as his mother, but close.

She wore blue jeans and an untucked white blouse, wrinkled across its bottom from being tucked in. She wiped her hand off on her thigh and held it out. He took it and she shook like a man would—like:

let's see who can squeeze harder.

She said her name was Kim White Owl, from the Warm Springs Reservation. "You guys are messy, huh? Hardly a clean dish in the house."

Elwood looked at the counter, where fruit flies swarmed around the pile of dirty dishes. Mostly he and his father ate off paper plates or over the sink, so they wouldn't have to wash anything.

"What's with your house?" she said. "What's with all this stuff?" She poured coffee into her cup—the sunflower cup his mother always drank from—and sort of toasted it at the walls, where the projectile points hung in fan-like displays, and then at the adjacent living room, where blood-red murals crowded every corner of wall, where beaded moccasins and a mortar-and-pestle and an at-latal and a dozen other artifacts covered the bookshelves and end tables.

"Is my dad here?"

"He went to get cinnamon rolls. He said you liked cinnamon rolls." She had this husky quality to her—a uniform layer of fat beneath which muscles moved—thatto Elwood made her seem equally suited for hard labor or tender sex. "So tell me, where'd you guys get all this stuff?"

"How long ago did my dad leave?"

"I don't know. Twenty, thirty minutes. Long enough for me to get dressed and make coffee and poke around." She slurped her coffee and sat down at the table and scooted a chair toward him with her bare foot. "Sit down, why don't you. Take a load off. You drink coffee?" He shook his head, no, and sat next to her. He could feel her eyes on him, but couldn't meet them. He concentrated instead on the rose-quartz deer skull, the way it sparkled under the sun shining through the window. "You're a handsome kid. You look a lot like your old man."

When she didn't say anything else, he said, "Thanks."

From the garage came the noise of the door rumbling up and the Bronco pulling in, and Kim said, "Speak of the devil."

They both stared at the far end of the kitchen, waiting for the door there to open, and when it did, Denis hurried in with a brown grocery bag clutched to his chest. "Hey," he said, his eyes jogging between them, settling on Elwood. "You're up."

An uncomfortable silence filled the kitchen, along with the smells of cinnamon and butter warming in the microwave, as Denis prepared their plates and poured orange juice and coffee. His war paint had faded and smeared so that his face looked bruised, shadowy.

He dropped a rolled-up newspaper on the table and Kim took the rubber band off it and spread it between her thumb and forefinger. She then let her head fall between her knees and whipped it back, grabbing her hair into a ponytail. This made her face appear even rounder.

She wants us to see her, Elwood thought. She wants us to see her clenched jaw and narrowed eyes, to know we're in trouble.

The microwave beeped and Denis pulled from it a steaming paper plate with three rolls on it. When he set one on Elwood's plate, and then on Kim's, she said,

"You know what I'd like to know?" Denis didn't answer, but kept his eyes on her. He knew something was coming—and then it came. "I'd like to know how two white boys ended up owning a bunch of museum-quality redskin shit they don't have any right owning." She said this softly, calmly, which made her seem all the more threatening, somehow.

Denis took a step away from her and said, "I don't know how to answer that." There were weird pauses in his speaking, as if he was out of breath.

She pointed a thick brown finger at him, and her face twisted into a scowl. "You better learn how to answer. You better learn." She began to punctuate every few words by stabbing her finger into the table. "Come tomorrow, I'm thinking you might have some elders and some tribal police asking some pretty serious fucking questions you better learn how to answer."

Elwood watched his father's hands ball into fists, and he wondered, would he strike her? But he only lowered his head, concentrating on his shoes.

Kim continued, the anger mounting in her voice. "I mean, what were you thinking? Bringing *me* here?" Elwood wondered the very same thing. "You *want* to get caught or something? Or you just so dumb and horny you hoped I wouldn't notice?" Here she put her hands to either side of her head, incredulous. "*Or* you think I'm going to be all, like, wow and shit. Like happy to see your little museum?" She snorted. "You gotta be kidding me." She jumped from her chair with such force it fell backward. "Where's my shoes? Where's my jacket?"

She walked in an aimless circle and then went to the

closet next to the staircase. She jerked it open and screamed. Sitting among the coats and boots was the dead Indian, snarling at them, monkey-like in its huddled brown shape.

She put a hand between her breasts, over her heart, as if to calm it. She seemed to spit at them when she spoke. "You dug up a grave?" She faced the closet again and stared at the thing. "What's wrong with you?" She examined the corpse another moment and then all of a sudden scooped it up and more ran than walked to the front door.

Denis hurried after her. "No! Leave that alone! Misty!"

She yanked open the front door and the house grew a little brighter. Stepping outside, she yelled over her shoulder, "Who you calling Misty? What the hell is wrong with you?"

Denis followed her outside, and Elwood followed him. The sky was cloudless, the air so bright everything seemed flat and bleached of color. A hot wind blew and ruffled their lawn's long grass, bending it flat, swirling it in ever-changing directions. Kim cut through it, moving toward her beater Ford pickup parked in the driveway.

"Give me the body," Denis said, his voice cracking with emotion. He grabbed the back of her shirt but she kept moving, even when it tore a little. "Please. *Please.*" He was begging her, and right then Elwood felt more than sorry for his father: he felt disgusted and embarrassed by him. "I'll give you money. As much as you want."

Kim reached the pickup and turned, a red flush burning through her brown skin, and at that moment, Elwood thought, if you sort of closed your eyes and made everything blurry, she looked *so* much like his mother it was creepy. "You're sick," she said. "You gotta let the dead rest."

Denis lunged at her and they began to wrestle with the corpse, their hands clasping it, tugging, and then—with a soft crack, like a popped knuckle—it broke in half. Chunks of skin and bone and the dust of decayed organs littered the driveway and they all gathered around staring at the mess, as it moved this way and that, blown by the wind, whirling and changing across the concrete so that it looked like some strange text, some hidden message left by the corpse
they would never understand.

The Iron Moth

I used to think Cairo, Oregon, was the only place in the world. This was when I was a kid, when the population was 6,000 and elk still crashed down from the mountains and wandered through our streets. Then the Californians moved up here and changed everything.

Used to be a white T-shirt, a pair of Wranglers, a belt buckle the size of a frying pan, a pair of shit-kickers, was standard uniform. Used to be the Golden Corral, with its $7.99 buffet, was everybody's idea of a quality supper. Now, not so much. Now, rather than *earning* your tan, moving irrigation pipe and bucking hay bales into a pickup bed all afternoon, you get inside some capsule that glows like a bug-zapper and has about the same effect in frying you to a crisp. Now, every time I turn around there's a new microbrewery or sushi joint or European car dealership, all of them springing up overnight like mushrooms.

Now most everybody who lives here is from someplace else.

I'm big. They call me Big Boy. Back in the heydays, some ten years ago, I was *the* star linebacker for the Mountain View Mountain Lions. I am six-foot-five, two hundred sixty pounds, with hands the size of T-bone steaks. Without much effort I can throw people around like cloth dolls, and I did.

I'm not proud of this but one time I hit my buddy Barney so hard his eye popped out. No kidding. This happened during practice, during a blitz drill, and I remember his eyeball hanging there by a red thread. Somehow we managed to shove it back inside him. I said, "Are you all right? Can you see?" and he blinked a few times before giving the thumbs up.

"As clear as mud," he said. To this day his left eye wanders as if possessed by its own strange life.

My senior year our twenty-man team went to state. That is the only time *that* has ever happened. Five busloads worth of locals drove to Portland to cheer us on, to shake their cowbells and scream bloody murder like the Romans in the gladiator movies. We lost—to a bunch of black boys—but it didn't matter.

We were heroes!

Believe it or not, not only was I good at football, I was one grade point short of salutatorian. University of Oregon, University of Washington, Oregon State, Washington State, all offered me scholarships, and in the end I decided to become a Duck. Everyone was absurdly happy. My parents bought me a Camero, custom-painted green and gold with the UO lettering stenciled across its hood. The sheriff bought me beer. The cheerleaders offered me blowjobs as if they were handshakes. Back then people *believed* in me. They thought I would make something of myself.

I didn't.

I remember my parents helping me move in to my dormitory. They had only left Central Oregon a handful of times and kept rubbing their eyes, commenting on the campus—"Look at that. Goodness, will you *look* at *that*."—as if surprised a life separate from Cairo actually existed outside a television set. They gave me many hugs, and before they left, my mother said, "The world is your oyster."

My entire life people have been saying things like this, throwing the weight of their dreams on me, and I always believed them. I believed with absolute certainty what lay in store for Big Boy was sunshine and go-go dancers and chocolate-chip cookies.

Not.

I liked the idea of college, the freedom of it. I could sleep all day, eat a Philly cheese-steak for breakfast, maybe go to class if I felt like it. For a few weeks I went nuts, all hot damn and rock 'n' roll, a girl in one hand, a Budweiser in the other, sweating my way through football practice, following the straight white powdered lines toward what I believed was a better life.

But I soon came to realize I was just another body here, no bigger or stronger—not really—than the fifty other guys on the roster, no smarter than the 10,000 other students on campus. Coaches and professors alike referred to me as "You!" Nobody knew who I was. Nobody cared. Always I felt Cairo's pull at the back of my neck, a blood-born gravity that made me pause and helped me understand: you want to be a Big Boy bad enough, you seek out the love that makes you such.

Knowing your place, it's called.

We don't say Cairo like you say Cairo. We say Kay-row.

At 3,000 feet above sea level, this is the high desert, a region known as Little Egypt. The name comes from the hundreds of miles of irrigation canals that zigzag every which way and bring lush alfalfa fields to soil that would otherwise hardly support the sage and fennel that grow native here.

It's a funny place, and if we gave prizes for funny behavior, we'd have to hand out an awful lot of them. Take for instance the annual Pigtona 500 race. Take the 4th of July cow-chip toss, the blindfolded lawnmower sprints, the Thanksgiving Rocking Chair Rock-A-Thon. Take the Deschutes County Rodeo: the opening ceremonies consist of cowboys racing their broncos to a marker, chugging three beers, then racing back, foaming at the mouth.

It's a Cairo thing.

The locals participate to remind themselves they are locals. And the Californians? They sometimes show up and laugh and point and snap photos like a bunch of half-assed anthropologists.

In the middle of town there is a cinder cone, several hundred feet high, with an asphalt road swirling up its side to the parking lot at its bald summit. This is Sphinx Butte. From here you feel like a god, with the whole world spread beneath you.

To the west are the Cascade Mountains, and in their shadow, Sisters and Bend and Redmond. To the east the horizon is ironed flat by the weight of the sky—long galloping horse-rides worth of desert that always make me think about shooting Indians and roping cattle, the whole rigmarole of cowboy bullcrap.

Here, every Saturday night, Barney and I shoot off anvils.

There is something truly beautiful about the sight. Picture a two-horned missile, spinning end over end, sometimes reaching heights up to 300 feet. When the sky is dark, when the anvil's base is warmed orange by two pounds of gunpowder, it is great fun tracking its haloed ascent into the blue-black sky, like some weird and dangerous comet that will eventually find its way back to me.

Many people—mostly old-timers—come and lay out their lawn chairs and picnic blankets and make low sounds of appreciation. Their faces are leathery from too much time spent in the sun, bailing hay and herding cattle and watching me lumber up and down a 100-yard stretch of carefully mowed grass. They crack the same old jokes—"What did your parents feed you growing up, Big Boy? Hay?"—and tell the same old stories—"You remember that time, that game against Crook County, when you put the quarterback in a coma?"

"Do I ever," I say.

Barney and I gather close to the launch site in order to fully appreciate the blast, a red-wreathed concussion that hits us square in the belly and foams Budweiser all over our knuckles. This is completely safe so long as nobody gets struck by the anvil or blown to smithereens by mishandled gunpowder.

We lean back our heads and smile and say, "Yee-doggies!" as the anvil rockets upward, as a gray-white cloud surrounds our bodies, stinking of sulfur. Then it is time to run. The distant sound of our screams lets us know our ears have been irrevocably damaged once again.

For the sake of perspective, you should know there are 7,000 grains in a pound of powder and just 30 grains in a .45 caliber bullet. Some 14,000 grains lit by a cigarette tip, that's something else! That's power!

You need two anvils to accomplish the feat, and the same as any relationship, their ignition works only if they are well matched. The lower anvil, it's not going anywhere. It's heavy-as-hell immovable, turned upside down with the natural cavity at its base exposed. A sleeve of high-strength steel, wherein I pour gunpowder and direct the fuse, lines this cavity. Next I lay a few playing cards over the powder hole. This helps build up pressure, acting as a gasket and a cushion on which to set the shooter anvil, a slimmer little number called The Iron Moth.

The Iron Moth is 150 pounds with the old Arm and Hammer trademark cast in relief on both sides. She is a beautiful machine.

I suck my cigarette until its cherry burns red. I touch the cherry to the fuse and the fuse spits out a spark and everybody holds their breath, waiting for the bang, the puff, the loud ringing that will linger in my head for days. The Iron Moth soars and cindered playing cards flutter all around us in a lonesome way.

Every time an anvil rises into the sky, Little Egypt listens. The ka-boom is inescapable. During the week, I will walk through Cairo and people will touch me on the elbow and report having heard the blast as far away as Redmond, some thirty miles distant.

"That's something else," I will say, smiling, knowing I am in Cairo's ears, even if I am no longer in their hearts.

You might wonder about a Mexican named Barney McCabe. I did. He is a half-breed. Half Mexican and half Irish—which makes him double Catholic—and for that I gave him a pretty hard time, back in fifth grade, when he first moved up here from Phoenix.

Before Barney, every Mexican I knew was Lopez or Suarez or something in the *ez* family. I told him as much and rather than sit me down and explain the intricacies of his genealogical history, he slapped me with the back of his hand—just like that—and with his finger in my face said, "You ever even *think* about making fun of me, fat boy, and I will stab a pencil into your eyeball."

That's Barney.

To this day no one has ever stood up to me—not my coach, not my father—*no*body except him. That was enough for me. We became serious friends. He has this royal air about him. He combs his hair back in a pompadour and always wears silky collared shirts with the top buttons unbuttoned, displaying his chest hair and a gold crucifix shaped like a knife.

The women are suckers for Barney. Partly for his body—he looks like he just stepped out of a Bowflex commercial—but mainly for his voice. On many occasions I have witnessed his accent at work. Women melt like dog shit on hot pavement. No joke. He could talk about anything—he could talk about eating a hamburger—and make it sound like the sexiest, most fascinating thing in the universe.

"And as I chewed this delicious ham-burger," he

would say, lingering on every syllable, while one of his eyes—the one I knocked loose—crept toward his nose, "it became ground up into little particles that descended into my stomach, where they were broken down by acids and made into *energy*."

I'm telling you: the special-effects blockbuster of the summer would not be more mesmerizing.

Some evenings, after we finish blasting anvils into the sky, after our audience filters away, if we don't feel like going to the bars, we set up our lawn chairs on Sphinx Butte and look out over Cairo with the blue haze of gunpowder still clinging to the air. A few cars remain in the parking lot—their windows dark and steamed over—and every once in a while a horn will beep, accidentally pressed by the elbow of some teenagers getting carried away. Otherwise we are alone to discuss matters.

"Japan," Barney says, only he says it like Huh-pan. "Korea. Thailand. I hear you can go there and make serious money teaching English."

I kill off a Budweiser, crush the empty, and reach into the cooler resting between us for another. "Seeing as you can barely speak English, let alone Japanese, I somehow doubt you're qualified, amigo." This is not true. I might have earned better grades, but Barney is the smart one. He keeps a dictionary in his bathroom and every day memorizes three new words while on the can. He could do great things, if only he put his mind to it. Certainly he could teach the pants off anyone—Japanese, Mongolian, Ethiopian, whatever—but I'm not going to tell him this. What are friends for if not for giving each other a good-natured ribbing?

He stares off into the darkness as if watching his dream play out on a screen there. "You don't even teach. Not really. You just engage them in conversation. They want practice, you see. Lawyers, doctors, businessmen. They pay you thirty dollar an hour just to bullshit with them."

For Barney, shit rhymes with feet.

"Heck, Barney," I say. "Sounds like you're qualified after all. Nobody I know is more full of bullshit than you."

"I'm talking serious money." He nods his head as if to muster conviction for the idea. "We should think about it."

"Yeah," I say. "Right."

Every day or two we come up with a new plan, a ticket out of town, something that will redeem us, that will lead us to greatness. We dream of white-sand beaches and jungle-safaris and oil fields and our minds hum with the green music of money. Next to women, it is our favorite topic of conversation—though for all our talk of travel, we have quite honestly not gone far.

Barney adjusts his chair so that he faces me and says, "What's with you today?" He holds up his hands, like: huh? "I do not like this grumpy monosyllabic thing you have going on right now."

Monosyllabic must have been one of his words of the day.

I am not grumpy. I am preoccupied. Today I learned from my boss who learned from his mother who learned from her neighbor who learned from the gas-station attendant Kelly Jones is coming home. Kelly Jones was my high school crush. She was prom queen, volleyball captain, student council president, ridiculously beautiful, and wanted nothing to do with me. She is red-haired and I have always been a chump for red-haired women. Ann Margaret makes me want to chew on my hand.

Kelly went off to college and married some financial analyst—and that was that. Sometimes I crack open the yearbook and stare at her perfect white teeth, but mostly I put her out of my mind, concentrating instead on the women at Pine Tavern, our favorite haunt, a locally famous dive with a pine tree sprouting through the floor and on past the ceiling. The women there look all right from a distance, but once you get close, you notice the acne scars and the wrinkles hiding behind their makeup, their makeup like the paint on a cellar door. They hurl darts and wear Daisy Duke short shorts and expect nothing except a couple drinks and a name-brand condom, and these days, that is all I have to offer.

But now Kelly Jones is getting a divorce—she is coming home—and I don't know what to think. Even when sitting down, I feel as if I am stumbling in a circle, groping the air for something to steady myself with…

Barney gives my shin a kick and says, "What's your deal? Where are you?"

"I'm here."

I consider telling him about Kelly, but don't. Freshman year they kissed in the back row of the movie theater—"Just messing around," Barney called it—and I have never forgiven him for this.

Now one of his eyes studies me while the other retreats back into his skull, seeking something there, and I try to make up for my inattentiveness by giving him one of my secret-joke looks. "You know what," I say, and he says, "What?" and I say, "I hope you appreciate the time we have spent together, because it won't be long now before I move into my deluxe chateau and spend all day lounging beside my swimming pool—and *then* you won't *ever* see me because I'll be too busy basking in all my glorious wealth."

Barney dismisses me with a wave. "Man, are you kidding me? That doesn't even compare to what I'll have going on." He makes a list with his fingers. "Yachts, mansions, an island in the South Pacific, a starring role opposite Angelina Jolie in her sexy new thriller."

For us, wishes come up in conversations like weather.

I say, "How about one of those *Sports Illustrated* swimsuit models for a maid?"

He toasts his beer and says, "Right on."

I ask will he run for president, will he throw the winning touchdown, will he perform brain surgery and accept his third Oscar all in the same afternoon?

He pretends to give this some serious thought before saying, "In all likelihood."

I say, "That would be the life."

The classic fantasy life of the loser, that is.

After that first semester, I didn't give up on college altogether. Along with Barney—who was, and still is, working full-time at the convenience store—I enrolled at Central Oregon Community College, a collection of buildings and hicks that's as worthlesly comical as its acronym: COCC.

COCC on the rock, everybody calls it.

I signed up for painting and creative writing—Poverty and Starvation 101, my dad called them—and more often than not did not attend. For a while, people still clung to me like a life preserver, believing me when I said I needed a break, a year to cool off, to save some cash and get my head together.

Then, as time went on, they stopped listening to the lie and I stopped telling it.

For the hell of it Barney and I signed up for a metal-smithing course. We were thrilled by the hammers and torches, the sweat and soot, our muscles aching as badly as our ears after we spent five hours in the shop, molding lumps of metal according to our own special vision.

Since then I have often thought *if only* the world were made of iron—a metal that can be drawn out, formed, machined, cast, laminated, hammered, inlaid, etched, punched, split, rolled, bent, chased, spun, welded, riveted, collared—*if only* that were the case, I might finally have the muscle, the sweeping muscle, to transform things, to right wrongs, to change the world.

If only.

Our professor told us way back when, blacksmiths periodically offered their anvils up to God—filling them with powder and blasting them into the sky like a sacrifice, seeking His favor, hoping He might bless them with wealth and happiness.

We thought that was pretty cool—a whole hell of a lot more interesting than the prayer we subjected ourselves to as kids—and soon thereafter Barney surprised me with The Iron Moth. He had wrapped a red ribbon around her horn. For the christening we used a bottle of Miller High Life, the champagne of beers.

We went seriously into anvil shooting after that.

A month after I dropped out of UO, I traded in my Camero for one of those tricked-out jacked-up Chevy pickups with the Cummins diesel engine. In its bed are fifty pounds of gunpowder sealed in a big plastic bucket, The Iron Moth, and some crumpled beer cans that rattle and clink when knocked around by the wind.

This fine June evening—that just-about twilight time when the air begins to blur—Barney and I are cruising up and down the strip, listening to the radio, honking the horn and yelling, "Hubba, hubba!" at all the pretty girls strolling around in peach tank-tops.

It's something to do.

My memory of Cairo and Cairo itself stand in such bizarre contrast I sometimes wonder if I spent my childhood in some computer simulation. Don't get me wrong: I don't altogether hate what has happened here. There is a sort of boomtown feel to the place that excites me. People flock here from all over—from Portland and San Francisco and LA—as if there is gold to be found. They are drawn to the skiing, the mountain-biking, the golf, the pure air, the big pines, all of them hungry for the same thing I am hungry for: the possibility of a better life.

This is what chugs through my mind when driving along Highway 126, halfway through town, halfway listening to Barney sing some Enrique Iglesias song around his cigarette. 126 is the road that rises up and over the Cascades, to Salem, our capital. Sometimes, rather than hanging a left onto my driveway with the weeds growing through the concrete, I imagine mashing the accelerator, continuing west.

A new life exists in that direction, along the road that ends at the capital building—its dome capped by a golden pioneer, dressed in buckskin, carrying a rifle, shining brilliantly, a beacon of the West.

A road can get a guy someplace, I think, imagining all the exits branching off this one, and me driving them, all the lives and adventures lying in wait, and then I notice the traffic ebbing and flowing around me, the souped-up pickups and the luxury sports cars, and I wonder, will I ever leave this place? Really?

We drive past Aubrey Butte—a golf-course community—past the revitalized downtown with its bistros and art galleries and sandblasted bricks reminding me of scabbed skin, past the new civic center where Shania Twain will play next week, past the new interstate under construction, past the new fast food joints, past the American Heritage Trailer Park, the suffering section of our manic depressive town—and then we turn around and do it all over again.

At the United Methodist Church, people throw rice at these happy smiling newlyweds, while across the street in the Moccasin Hollow Graveyard four guys in black suits carry a coffin toward a hole in the ground followed by a herd of mourners.

Everything is mixed up.

Take for instance the really real locals, the beer-bellied anti-intellectuals who wear seed caps or NASCAR caps, their jaws humped out with dip, while the lentil-eating Californians creep along in their boat shoes and platinum dye-jobs, making out they are pretty by the way they walk, spending money just because they get tired of carrying it around.

Truth be told, these rich guys are the ones who ought to be wearing NASCAR. NASCAR says it all —upholstering yourself with brand names, feeling special only because some other boob is playing catch-up in the rearview mirror.

I roll down the window and fill the truck with a dry hot wind. I breathe the animal smells of bacon and barbeque mixed with sage and dust and perfume and when I exhale, it is with the sense of knowing my place and knowing it doesn't feel quite right, somehow.

I work at Big R.

Whatever you need, Big R's got it—as their jingle goes—feed and tackle, knives, Justin boots and Stetson hats, lawn equipment, power tools, gas and charcoal grills, hunting blinds, decoy ducks, bows and rifles, etc. Most important of all, we are a class-C vending area, which means my gunpowder needs are well served by the 30% employee discount.

Today I am selling fishing licenses to fathers and sons who wear dorky khaki vests with many compartments. I ask will today be the day? Are they going to catch the big one? They say, "You got that right!" and I can practically hear them salivating as they imagine the taste of trout, peppered filets drowned in lemon and hissing on the barbeque.

I am leaning against the counter, my chin in my hand, daydreaming my way into this job my cousin called about the other day—a $25,000 job on a Portland construction crew he is contracting —when I hear a voice say, "Augustus? Right?"

Nobody has called me *that* in a long time—not for years—and it takes a moment for the fog to clear, for the name to register and the speaker to materialize. Standing nearby, wearing a mint-white polo shirt that matches her smiling teeth, is none other than Kelly Jones.

I nearly fall over.

I say, "Kelly!" For a second I stand there with my arms sort of half-raised—I don't know what to do with them—then I stick my hand out for a shake she receives. "Kelly," I say again and pump her tiny hand, so warm and thin-boned, like a bird seized from the air. "My!"

Her smile grows a little wider. "I guess you remember me then?"

"Of course I remember you, Kelly." I let her hand go and she wipes it on her skirt and I grow suddenly self-conscious. Am I sweaty? Did I wash my hands after I went to the can?

I move around the counter with all the grace of a bulldozer, wanting to be closer to her, and she takes several steps back. I realize what I must look like to her, like something out of *Animal Planet*. In scale with my gorilla-like body, she might be a banana, a banana I am genuinely starved for.

There is a friendly silence between us. Like an idiot I nod my head and wait for something, *any*thing, to come to mind. "Kelly," I say again, and then, before I can stop myself, I punch her in the shoulder and say, "Kelly Jones! How about that?"

She keeps smiling but I can see the humor fading from her face as she holds the place where I punched her and says, "Ow."

"Oh," I say. "Oops. Sorry." I laugh wretchedly and shrug and shake my head. "Guess I don't know my own strength."

"No, I guess not."

I catch a whiff of her perfume—apricots and honey with a musky *under*smell—and recognize it as the same she wore in high school. I remember walking past her in the halls, breathing deep from the sweet puff of air that followed her. How good it feels to have her inside my lungs again. The sensation is similar to hearing an old song on the radio. One you loved but forgot existed. Rediscovering it makes you happy.

She says, "What are you up to these days?"

"Not much." I make a broad gesture with my hand that indicates the store. "Working, you know. Same old. I've got a little blacksmith operation I've been running on the side." This is not entirely untrue. "Life is good." This is not entirely true.

She says, "Is that where you got your scar?" and I say, "Huh? Scar?"

Back in the day she met my small talk with the smallest talk you can have. "Yes," for instance, and "No." Mainly "No," such as when I asked her to slow-dance at Homecoming. In all our life, I suppose we have exchanged maybe fifty words, which is why I am somewhere between "Thank God!" and "Oh, Lord!" when suddenly confronted with all her friendly chatter.

"Your scar?" She points at my forearm, where the tissue is all gummed up and discolored like play-dough left too long in the sun. "Did you get that from blacksmithing? It's pretty nasty."

"Oh, that?" I touch it, remembering. "That's from foolishness."

One day, senior year of high school, I was in shop when a sudden storm of hail made the world as white as winter in five minutes. This was April or May and I remember watching Kelly through the window when she ran outside with her girlfriends—all of them wearing their shorts and T-shirts—packing the hail into balls and throwing them, rolling around on the ground, laughing, while the sun came from behind the clouds and brought the world back into spring again. Everything steamed and she looked to me like some sort of desert oasis, too good to be real.

At the time I was using a circular saw to cut a cheeseboard for my mother. The blade hit a knot, I slipped, and my skin opened as easy as a zipper.

"How about let's forget about me," I say. "How are *you*?"

Her eyes do a shifty thing, "Honestly, things aren't so good." Her voice now has an edge that could cut anything it came against. For a moment she appears to be swallowing needles—then her face brightens. "But I'm glad to be home."

Like an idiot I say the same thing my grandmother said to me when I returned from UO: "It's always nice to come home."

Barney and I have spoken earnestly of opening a shop called Traditional Ironworks. We would specialize in foundering horses and corrective shoeing and once our reputation spread from the ranches of Oregon, we imagine getting called to Texas and to Montana and maybe we would even travel as far as the sheikdoms of the Middle East to bless the world with our iron genius. Imagine it! Flying in a private twin-engine plane, from horse to horse!

For now, we work out of my single-car garage attached to my one-bedroom rental, a shotgun shack with shag carpeting the color of Velveeta cheese and mice scuttling through the walls. I moved in here after mydad sat me down and told me he was quite frankly worried. "I just want you to make something of yourself," he said. "Anything." I could tell this admission took a lot out of him. The blood was gone from his face and there were dark half-moons of sweat growing from his armpits. A week later I moved out, not wanting to hurt him more than I already had.

This blacksmithing operation is what you might call a step in the right direction. Sometimes we cold call the ranches, hunting for clients, but mostly, sadly, our orders come from family and friends who feel sorry for us.

Ever since I ran into Kelly I cannot stop gritting my teeth, cracking my neck, throwing pretend punches at imaginary villains. I feel like I used to feel game-time, when I settled into a three-point stance and stared eye-to-eye with some rhinoceros, ready to skin my knuckles against his teeth, my blood lava-hot.

I find an outlet at the forge, pumping the bellows, spitting on the coals for the sexed-up steam noise. "It's always nice to come home," I say and slap my forehead and say over and over again, "It's always nice to come home." It seems like the stupidest thing in the world to say. "Jesus."

When the coals are good and hot I climb up in the pickup bed and drag the Iron Moth toward the tailgate. The other night was unkind to her. I rub a palm across her damaged horn—blunted, its tip slightly cracked—and right then Barney pulls into the driveway in this purple Lincoln the length of your average sperm whale. He toots the horn and kicks open the door and says, "Que pasa, Big Boy?"

"Nada," I say. "Now give me a hand with this thing, will you?"

Together we hustle The Iron Moth over to the forge. By now the coal is ready and smells how I imagine a nighttime city would. I apply heat to The Iron Moth until her horn glows a bright orange. We forge out the blemishes using a sledge and rounding hammer, then apply a final polish with the Scotch Brite disc, scrubbing until I can see my face in the metal. There is a pink sootiness to me that would be natural in a firepit but not in a person's skin.

Gradually my desire lessens. No better antidote than sweat. I stare into the red nowhere of the coals, wanting so badly everything in particular.

"Guess what I heard today?" Barney says, "I heard Kelly Jones got a divorce and is back in Cairo. Can you believe that, man? Kelly Jones and her Jelly Kones." He shakes his body like a hula girl and laughs, no doubt thinking about how she looked in her volleyball shorts and sports bra, when her sweat brightened under the gym lights, making her sparkle.

I pick up the sledgehammer and sling it to my shoulder, where it rests, like an unsaid threat. "Is that right?" My voice pretends only a vague interest. "Hmm."

"You used to like her, no? Back in high school?"

"I don't really recall," I say. "High school was a long time ago."

That night I dream of shoving my intestines full of black powder, lighting a match, so I might rise like an anvil, orange fire snapping from my ass, my body rocketing so high the blue sky would fade into stars, all the way to the moon. To the moon!

When I wake I feel as though I have fallen from a great height. I lay in bed for a long time and in the soft morning light, I feel Kelly, somewhere nearby, like a raised hand shadowing my mind, like a reminder of everything I always wanted but never achieved.

I buy flowers. I buy chocolates. I go to JC Penney with the intention of buying a suit. The salesman—who is not from around here and who smells like he just rubbed himself with a Cosmopolitan magazine—takes one look at my Carhartt jacket and blue-jeans and says, "Well."

"Well?" I say, "Well, what?"

Think of a yellow dog that is puny and ugly but fancies itself the greatest dog in the whole world and you have this salesman. He says, "May I ask what's the occasion?"

"Who says there's an occasion?
Christ, can't a guy just buy a suit?"

"Right," he says and clucks his tongue three times, studying me. "You'll probably want to try the Big and Tall store. We don't carry your size. You won't fit into anything."

The moon is full, coloring the neighborhood a strange hue. It makes the houses look brighter, more vibrant than they really are, and it makes my skin look as gray and bleak as a cadaver's. A breeze blows, bringing good smells with it, of charcoal and sweet summer sage. It is a beautiful night.

I am wearing a collared shirt and a clip-on tie and khaki pants—all brand-new, all bought from the Big and Tall—and I am hunkered down behind the bushes in front of Kelly Jones's parent's house. Not because I am some sort of pervert, but because Barney's purple Lincoln is parked out front and I want to know what the hell is going on.

The kitchen window is an orange square of light. Inside it Barney and Kelly drink from bottles of beer. I don't know what to think. Seeing them together, touching, their mouths moving, I am too stunned for thought.

Like the slick scum-sucking son of a bitch that he is, Barney reaches over and tucks her hair behind her ear, his fingers lingering there a second, just long enough so her smell, her apricot smell, no doubt clings to him. She smiles and he says something and her smile erupts into a laugh.

I want to swallow gasoline and belch fire.

Her eyes rise and meet mine. Though she sees nothing but her own reflection, I feel convinced she *senses* me. And she is talking to me, her hands rising into a palms-up wave I can't figure out, gesturing hello, maybe, or *stop, stay away*.

I drive west on Highway 126, toward the Cascades, toward Portland, the road disappearing beneath my tires like a rug jerked from beneath me. I have the radio going at top volume. On the honky-tonk station a fiddler saws a song that reminds me of the mournful music of coyotes. An owl swoops before my headlights—its belly a flash of white—chasing something, narrowly avoiding my grill. The speedometer reads 70, 80, 90 and the engine roars and my blood fizzes as I seek escape, headed for a brand-new world where I might once again discover a thing like hope.

Cars and semis emerge from the darkness, zipping along the eastbound lanes. When their headlights spotlight me, I study my reflection in the rearview mirror and see a weird gray face dappled with the shadows of splattered dead bugs.

This desperate momentum doesn't last long.

The Cascades rise before me like a fence that I climb and climb until I reach the saddle between Jefferson and the North Sister, right before the highway descends into the alpine forests that will eventually give way to the blue water and green grass of the Willamette Valley.

Here I feel what an anvil must feel when it pauses at the peak of its ascent—a tug, a realization that I cannot in fact fly. And I can only wonder, how great will the crater be when I come back down to meet the earth?

My boot eases off the accelerator and I park along

the shoulder and click on my hazards. An anemic yellow flashes and flashes, brightening the black highway that coils off into the distance like a snake without end. There lies the potential beginning of something new, something inviting, something better, I think.

Off in the distance a road-killed raccoon seems to grin at me, like: if only you had the balls.

Eventually I swing a U-turn and downshift my way back through the trees and the darkness, toward the welcoming lights of home.

Midnight, and I am alone, standing on top of Sphinx Butte, sipping a Budweiser, wearing my old letterman jacket. It still fits beautifully. All of Cairo sprawls beneath me, its streetlamps and windows lit up and surrounding patches of blackness. Headlights move along the streets and highways, as thick as sperm, some injecting themselves into garages and parking lots, some spreading out into the countryside.

And I remember how I was once happy there, in a place that is no longer mine.

I fire a match and spark the fuse and step away from The Iron Moth. A moment later a red wreath of light bursts from her bottom. My ears pop, my hair stirs, and the two horned missile, the Iron Moth, rises into the black sky—a phantom net flecked with throbbing stars—where I momentarily lose her.

The Language of Elk

Evenings, when the sky goes pink and the shadows melt together, you'll hear it—so low and sad and frightening, a dark sound rising from a dark place, the deepest corner of lung, nested there like a secret. If your back is turned to the forest from which it pours, you'll turn around—quick—finding strength in the tight handshake of the walnut stock of your thirty-aught-six. Listen: a low-throated moan, faraway, copied by another, closer by, then another, then another.

This is the language of elk.

I listen nightly. Come sunset, I peel off my socks and dry my feet on the wrinkled porch boards, drinking a Coors or three between sucks of pipe while enjoying the rumbling sounds of my beasts, my elk. I own them. They are mine. For twenty years they have chewed my grass and huckleberry and died and become my soil.

Inside, Willow bangs pots together, makes kitchen noises. What was supper still sticks to the air—tortillas wrapped around grilled poblano stuffed with burger—soon fading into the piney breeze. If I ask, she will bring me another beer. She is good in this way and many others, but still we are not right. Way back, we used to be a beautiful piece of marriage—you'd look at us and smile and want to rub our bodies for luck.

Now a daughter bleeds a wound between us.

To the west the Cascade Mountains make a starless

space in the sky, toothy and black, their many glaciers glowing gray in the moonlight. They have been there forever. They—along with this twilight chorus of elk—make me feel young and tender. I stare at those old leviathans and am reminded how beetles and worms will one day tunnel their way through me.

When my thumbnail scrapes away the skins of three or four beer labels—which I fold neatly and put in my pocket—when the sky goes full dark, when a yawn stretches my mouth, I know it is time to say goodnight to the elk. I do this with my fists lifted above my head, like some weird benediction in this ceremony of wilderness.

"Welcome to Foder Ranch," I say. "I'm Pete Foder."

If they are too clean and look like the city—Portland—I will liquefy my vowels, heighten my twang for drama. We will exchange muscular handshakes. We will talk of the weather and look at the sky.

Their rifles are new and shiny, just like their cars, their engines ticking out near the corrals. We tour the cabins and the dining hall, and I point—*this* is where you sleep, *this* is where you eat, *this* is where we butcher your kill—my finger stabbing the air with an authority that partners ritual: I have done this every week: I will continue to do this every week. When there is little left to say, I might spit a slug of mucus and then we will watch, silently, as it disappears into the hungry suck of dust.

"See you at supper," I say and nod and square my hat.

Ask me about my daughter, Sonora, and I will turn my eyes elsewhere. Ask me why she crouches in her room all day and rocks on her heels, and I won't take the trouble to even shrug. Ask about why she won't make words. Ask about drool. Ask about the faraway look to her face…I don't know.

My wife has Mexican blood in her. You can see it in her cheekbones, in her inkblack hair, in her broad and thoughtful face. We named our daughter Sonora. Sonora is a Spanish word. It means pretty sound. She brings a hiccup to my heart, tugs me in and out of love.

Late at night when the cabin sleeps, I sometimes stand above their beds and put out a hand, wanting very badly to touch my girls. My hand hovers over their faces, feeling the heat of their breath, and I think about the life pumping below: it belongs to me—either by bloodwork or legal certificate—and I want to touch their lips and stroke their hair and hug them tight. I want to make our closeness real.

But my hand—husked with callus and pretty hairy—trembles above these female things, stinging against their heated breath as if brought in from the snow. They are a part of my life—but only make me more alone, seems like.

I hug my pillow on the way to sleep. I have little dreams about how happy we are, nice hugs, holding hands in Indian paintbrush meadows.

It is Saturday, dawn. The air tastes clean and cold and every footstep over pine needle whispers like a broomstroke. Showerwater chills in my hair, my jeans fit warmly from resting on the stove. I love those morning mountains, bearded with forest and banded with sediment and stained red from the red sky that matches the red bark of lodgepole pine.

I have a chipped mug in my hand that reads "Pete's Joe." From it I sip sugared coffee and in the same motion check my wristwatch. Fifteen more minutes will mark 6:30, chow time. Custom demands I rattle the iron triangle while the hunters herd into the dining hall. This, the iron triangle, makes them feel like real cowboys.

In the mean time I knock on cabin doors, say rise and shine, and listen to my clients grunt and shuffle around, getting out of bed to stir the stove's embers, to toss on another log and struggle into their wool socks and blue jeans. I imagine them making their beds and then laying down their rifles on the rough Pendleton blanket.

How slick and beautiful the rifle looks to them, its barrel creasing the pillow, bleeding a drop of oil on white. These men, with their soft hands and soft bellies, crouch down as if in prayer and smile and stretch out their fingers, caressing the gunmetal slowly, delicately, like a lover—the pucker of the bore, big enough to stick their pinky inside. Still hazy from sleep, their eyes shutter closed as they whisper luck into their bullets, imagining a trophy rack to hang in their den, something to brag about to the neighbors while sipping cocktails next to elk-steaks sizzling on the grill.

Then it is 6:30 and I rattle the iron triangle—its metal sounding so foreign in the morning hush—and my clients rub their tiny dreams from their eyes and step out in the cold and stamp their brand-new boots and slap each other on the back and talk loud because today they plan on killing. This is exciting. From the collective grin on their lips, breath steams the air like something boiling over.

Breakfast is fresh huckleberries, biscuits drowned in gravy of the deepest gray, butter melting all over your muffin, bacon, hot coffee. Willow stands ghostly behind the steam of the buffet line, halfway flirting with a man who is as black as a blackbird and wearing a gold watch. She says, "If there's anything you need, holler." Her teeth flash in a smile and the black guy copies the gesture before taking his tray to find a seat.

I rub my beard and think about how long it has been since I last kissed that smile. Months, if you can believe it. Our distance has become ritual. Somewhere along the line, work became a precedent and love got pushed in the closet, food for the moths. My mind chugs through our history, trying to make sense, trying to understand the effect of a wrong child.

Our dining hall is something famous. Discovery Channel has been here, along with *Outdoor Life*, *Field and Stream*, *Guns and Ammo*, even *Better Homes and Gardens*, *Better Homes and Gardens* referring to it as "Neo-gothic" in their October issue featuring America's creepiest buildings.

This is the Oregon equivalent of George Washington Slept Here.

Willow and I built it mostly from logs but the skeletons are what make it special. Take for instance the shaved elk-bone rods fitted into tables, dead lumber, their heavily lacquered surface grayish and uneven so you have to be careful and keep your coffee steady on its tray. Braiding the pillars and crossbeams are fangs and molars and claws. Along the west wall—dividing the kitchen from the dining area—is a counter made entirely of vertebrae, fitted together like some morbid puzzle. There are antler chandeliers and bullhorn chairs and a cougar mounted on a log and next to it five pheasants frozen in flight. Elsewhere in the room you can find a collection of signal horns and powder horns and antique rifles and hunting knives with elk-foot handles. The walls are crowded with nearly fifty skull-and-rack mounts of deer and elk and antelope and one boar and two moose. Hanging among them is an enormous grizzlybearskin with its claws and its head attached, its face to the floor, its jaw propped open in a mute snarl. It looks as if it has been hurled against the wall at a great velocity and flattened there like in the cartoons. The fur is a deep cinnamon with silver highlights along its hump.

Alone in the corner is the skeleton from which it came. For two weeks I wired and bolted and glued its bones together in a pose meant to be frightening. It balances on its haunches with its forelegs stretched above its skull as if to scratch the ceiling. A brass plate on its foundation details the Boone and Crockett Club score of 550.35. No record-breaker but damn big.

I killed these things. I built this place. It is mine. I drum a thumbnail along the edge of a table and feel reassured: my hands pulled the trigger and forked the meat and reconstructed the skeleton: my hands put all this together and could just as easily take it apart.

I walk among my clients with a cowboy swagger, my thumbs hooked in my belt. I feel their eyes crawling all over me, these three businessmen in pristine Stesons. One of them is trying to grow a ridiculous mustache. He grabs my wrist and asks a bunch of questions—I say, "Nine hundred acres, six hundred elk, a pond, a river, horses, and enough woods to choke every beaver in Oregon."

They want stories, so I develop a dramatic deepness to my voice and say, "See this coat? I'll tell you about this coat. Shot and skinned and tanned some three years ago."

I explain how I humped its meat from the depths of the Ochoco Valley. They want to touch the leather—as if to draw some power from it—and I let them.

They say, "Tell us about *after* you shoot, Pete. The cleaning part."

I say, "You want to know about cleaning? I'll tell you about cleaning."

I unsheathe my bowie knife and lay it on the table, its silver blade oranged by the sunlight leaking through the window. I lean my face real close and detail taking apart an animal. First puncture behind the hamstring and hang the elk high from a sturdy pine. Now listen while I surgeon with words, sawing from ass to sternum, the incision so neat. Step back and watch unzipped veins bleed the ground muddy. Okay? Now put your fingers in the wound, the flesh slippery and warm, and peel back the skin and listen to it make a noise you associate with electricity. In the belly spiralized guts rest encased in a foggy gutsack. Here are the innards, colored and bound like wet balls of yarn. Place them aside for the flies and yellow jackets. The hatchets of bladebones, a joint's rubbery ligature, I dig deeper and deeper through the red strata, detailing the archaeology of gore.

Which they love. You can tell by their eyes getting bigger and bigger, the way their spoons hover forgotten before their mouths.

I pick up my knife and cut the air and say *this* is how you flay the muscle into small red strips that grow blue with the bluebottle blackfly. Stack the meat into pyramids for later, for salting and smoking, and now only a loose hide remains, which you would clean and tan and oil and if you were an Indian make soft by chewing.

When I finish my speech I reach out and stab a huckleberry off the black guy's plate. I eye it a second, balanced on the blade, before my teeth bite down and the huckleberry pops and the men look at me sideways as if I am something naked and dangerous. None of them says a word. The black guy pokes at his biscuit.

Outside the day is bright and wonderful.

Many years ago the Oregon Department of Fish and Wildlife created a Cascade hunt. Meaning for seven days and seven days only during the third week of October you could pay for a general season hunt with unlimited entry, along with the thousands of other archery, muzzleloader and centerfire rifle hunters trying to intercept the elk migrating to their winter range. ODFW categorizes elk by watershed district. In some districts any bull with a visible antler is legal. In others it must be branched. To the east of the Cascades—my neck of the woods—you got the Deschutes, Metolius, Fort Rock, Grizzly and Sprague units, all mainly contained within the Deschutes Watershed District.

Foder Ranch might be premium hunting territory smack in the middle of this very district, but its bureaucrats in khaki uniforms can't tell me boo. They try but can't. One time I chased them down the driveway with a chainsaw when they dropped hints about cutting my fences, baiting the elk off my land and onto theirs.

"You're overpopulating your range," was what they said. "You're way over your carrying capacity. It won't be long before some parasite or disease wipes out the herd."

I figure them for being anally retentive to the hundredth degree since I let folks hunt *whenever* with no horn regulations—no regulations period—no permits, no licenses, nothing but a low-impact good time where you are guaranteed to kill an elk, bull or cow, whatever your fancy.

You shoot a cow, for a small fee, I could turn it into a bull. I am quite the taxidermist. When the elk cast their horns in January, I gather them up to add to the Elkhorn Steeple. This is a mound thirty feet in diameter at its base, tapering gradually to a rounded top over twenty feet high and looking a lot like Mount Bachelor. There must be a thousand antlers in the Steeple. From it I choose a nice pair to mount onto your cow so your neighbor would be impressed enough to whistle at it.

Never a dissatisfied customer.

What's more, I can smoke your rawhide to soften the skin and darken its color. I can cut it up and sew it back together, making moccasins for the entire family, dresses for the wife, and for the great white hunter: a ceremonial robe with a pictographic narrative of your weekend at the ranch.

Without fences, elk are migratory animals. To kill them you have to know where to look. Most people don't know where to look. Last year the hunter success rate was three percent in the Upper Deschutes Unit, three percent in the Metolius Unit, two percent in the Fort Rock Unit. That translates to a lot of money and time and energy banked on shit odds.

The hunter success rate at Foder Ranch was 100 percent.

Listen: You think hunting at a 45-degree angle is exhausting, try skinning and quartering an 800-pound elk. The real work starts once the animal is dead. Does the ODFW take care of that? They do not. I take care of that.

No wonder I am such a success. People—pathetic people mainly—will pay through the nose for this sort of thing. They put down their $5,000 and they expect a trophy delivered to them on a silver platter with a nice pine garnish. I do my best to deliver the product.

Fish in a barrel, it's called.

I sit on the porch—drinking Coors, breathing pipe-smoke—while off toward the cabins my men celebrate around a campfire. The flames shoot high, eating the dry October wood, sparks swirling up into the night sky, while a bottle of dark liquor is passed and suckled. There is always a bottle. It sets them apart as hunters, and as men.

They have forgotten about make-upped wives,

grubless lawns, golf, patio furniture. By way of slaughter, they feel new, like something birthed and aborted by the same prick of lead. Just listen to them, hooting like apes, slapping each other high fives and telling hunting stories with voices full of accents more distinguished than my own.

I have them pegged for being happy in that special middle-aged succeeded-at-everything way. They come from streets called Bear Brooke Lane, neighborhoods called Horse Back Butte, Aubrey Glen, Swan Hollow, places that don't live up to the promise of their names. For these guys, nature is a foreign thing. They see an eagle and feel a surge of American pride, an urge to send Priority Mail, or whatever. Funny how they go and shoot *one* animal and all of a sudden consider themselves card-carrying members of the Davy Crockett bloodline.

I wash beer down my throat and massage my hands—cramped from butchering—my fingernails rimmed rusty with blood, and then, hearing my name, I lean forward with interest. They begin to talk about me in hushed tones, the way I hauled a hundred-pound hindquarter over my shoulder, grinning under the lacquered red as if it were candy. They are impressed. The black guy calls me, A True American Man.

They all of a sudden fall quiet when Mangold lets out a moan—so deep and lonely and rising from his corral, filling the night, rumbling under my skin to make it pimple.

Mangold is my stud bull, the breeder of my darlings, the granddaddy elk of Foder Ranch, with a rack that branches upward like so many fingers. Late summer into fall, one by one, I march the cows into his corral, where they sniff the air and flutter their ears before bending their necks to chew alfalfa. Mangold wastes no time with pillow talk. For a second or two, he climbs on their backs and grunts and pulses and then the deed is done—and then the cow pulls away and turns to look at him as if curious what just happened.

For nearly ten years this has been his life. His beard has faded into a silvery hue, like mine, its golden luster lost. Soon I will have to set him loose. His arthritis prevents the slick application of his manhood and his daughters have become his lovers and for sake of quality breeding, I will have to set him loose and then he will find peace before the stare of some suburbanite's muzzle.

The men take off their Stetsons as if in church, their eyes rolling around in their heads, as they listen to Mangold lowing some miserable song. From the secret cavities of the forest there sounds another elk, then another. Their lowing is like some strange vapor released from the earth—the noise of which reminds us of our delicacy and newness in this ancient empire of stone and tree and jaw.

The men look over their shoulders, into the forest, imagining all the dark things hidden there. The whiskey wears off and their smiles straighten into a thin set of lips. The wind rises and a trail of embers blows from the firepit, across the ground, breezing away to disappear and eventually become part of the night.

Let me tell you about my daughter, Sonora. She is round-faced and beautiful like her mother, with the same brown eyes, their brown broken up by chips of yellow. When she stares, so intense and unblinking, you would by God think she was making a Polaroid. To tell you the truth, it's creepy. The talking part of her is down in some deep cave of her nature, hidden from the world. But she can sing in a way that makes you believe in heaven. Just about all day she sits in front of the radio, tuned-in to the honky-tonk stations, all steel guitars and voices drawling their truckstop sorrow.

I remember her as a baby—that same dark-eyed stare peeking from under her cornsilk hair. She never cried, even when learning her legs, falling on her butt a lot. Back then I held her in my arms and felt like a hero. Then came two-years-old and she started humming along with our record player—but wouldn't even call me *daddy*. She stared at the wall for hours. Still does. Sometimes she'll slap herself and tear at her hair and we'll put on Hank Williams to soothe her into hums and song.

The doctor said, "Autistic," and he must have liked the way word tasted on his tongue because he said it what seemed like a thousand times. He said it so many times it stuck and stayed true and there was no fixing her, nothing I could do.

I love her. But she makes me feel like I need to prove something. What makes me proud, at least, is that she has a gift, like many of her kind: a pitchperfect gift. She is crippled in the head but brilliant of throat. She is a singing little fool. She could sing all day and sometimes she does. I put an ear to her bedroom door and listen to her songs and want to make it like it was before—to rock her in the cradle of my arms—but she doesn't like to be touched and I don't have the courage to try to convince her otherwise.

My love is a thing of distance. Like looking through the wrong end of a rifle's scope. I can reach out and feel her skin—but she remains so far away.

The spice of hay and animal fills up our heads like strange advice. I take my clients—a gang of computer folk—through the holding pens and show them the calves. I say, "Put out your thumb. They'll suck on it like a nipple." And the men do. And the men smile in a bedroom sort of way.

My Mexicans tip their John Deere caps as they fill up the grain troughs. "Good job, amigos," I tell them and hitch my belt, fitting some warm straw along the corner of my mouth.

One of my clients, Mr. Computer, scrunches up his face and lets loose a sneeze and asks if I've got a namefor this cute little elk sucking his thumb. I say, "Nope." I try to keep my distance. I breed the animals, but I don't mother them. In my book they're already dead—they're meat—so why bother?

It's hard not to feel responsible. It's hard—when the mere sight of family makes my heart beat a pace quicker—not to feel like it could have been different. Sometimes I wonder if I made my daughter wrong. Through eleven years of cold distance, Willow has tried to help me recognize this.

Here is the story of Sonora's conception:

Outside Vancouver, my buddies and me hunted

bear. Everyday we woke before sunrise—the fog and the darkness curling around our boots—and set off in different directions with our rifles strapped to our backs. No dogs, just bullets. I was straddling timberline when the griz untangled itself from a manzanita thicket, lean and blond with a low rumble pouring from its mouth. I brought my .338 to my shoulder and aimed down its chamber as the bear showed off teeth the size of fingers nested in purple gums, and shambled forward, its fur trembling.

It took three bullets to turn its charge and two hours later I tracked it to a cave with ice and blood around the entrance and no way in hell was I going in there, so I smoked it out. I doused with whiskey a pile of pine and before long the bear shot from the cave with blood and sweat steaming off its spiked fur.

One more bullet was all it took.

That night I was wild with gore and liquor, something beastly. In the tent I found Willow and we made our pact in the dark, fast and hard, and she was a victim beneath my system of limbs. I remember her screaming no, no, *no*. I remember her little fists. But I couldn't stop, and beneath her skin, my violence must have imprinted something wrong.

She said it was like a monster, the tearing inside. Then came Sonora and eleven years of not being able to make things better.

My pipe bowl has gone cold but I pretend to smoke anyway, a column of steam drifting from my mouth, making the moon a silver smear. Stars wink down their quartzite shine and tomorrow men will come to scavenge my woods. The aspen and the birch have turned with autumn, their gold-coin leaves interrupting the vast wash of evergreen. A frost varnishes the forest floor. I snuggle down in my coat and listen to the elk in a half-trance, sleepy in my beer, lulled by their haunting timbre.

Then I hear the blow of something sweet and soprano and foreign, like some enchanted flute. My eyes get wide as I recognize it as the prettiest sound I have ever known—Sonora.

I jump from my rocker and cup a palm to my ear. For the space of a minute I listen to the trees whisper—and then the quiet breaks into a high-pitched moan. Sonora is outside. I hurry down the steps, along the gravel path, toward the corrals. She belts out another call, as deep as her vocal cords can manage, and this time the elk answer: the forest erupts in low-throated chorus and I duck my head and shrink a little.

I hold my penlight before me like a weapon, stabbing the dark with its yellow beam. In the corral I find Mangold, motionless as a waxwork, his antlers veining up into the dark. And upon him lays my daughter, limp across his back, his hump a pillow for her head. I see her breath ghosting the air, her eyes glowing, yellow and brown grains snowing through them, lidless in their stare, telling me nothing. I step forward and she shows her teeth in a snarl. She will bite me. Of this I am certain.

I stand there awhile and don't know what to do—my hand opening and closing into a helpless fist. Finally I tell her to get down—get down *now*—before Mangold hurts her. She sits upright and points at me and makes her mouth into an O—out of which pours the most horrible banshee cry.

I shiver. My body feels lost.

The next day I drink my way through a cooler of beer. By evening I am wagging my finger at the Cascades, saying, "You make perfect sense!"

The Cascades are *always exactly* the same. Even if I turn around in a circle or swear or shake my fist at them, they won't care. Not like frigid wives or freaky daughters. The Cascades don't blame or hate or love or give a flying fuck. Things eat and fight and screw and die and who cares? Not the Cascades. They are BIG! They are reddish in the mornings—as if capillaried with blood—bluish in the twilight—like smoke ghosting into the dark. They happened so long ago. They happened before emotion. They happened before words—though the language of elk seems a fitting voice: old and strong and singing from the cavities of its woods.

The fibers and pipes of my system relax, my bloodstream a cool gray calm I wouldn't mind pouring in a pitcher to take a sip of. I settle for another swig of beer. Clouds slide along and the mountains cut right through them and I rock in my rocker with beer labels scattered about my feet like wood shavings.

Full dark, I wake up to Mangold lowing, a big block of air flooded with bass, coiling around the cabin, taking my hand and leading me off the porch and to the corral, wher enough, there she is, on top his back.

I lean ag e fencepost and rub the sleep from my eyes and awhile in the moonlight. Her lips move—with question—her lips make *words*. I shake away the fuzz in my head and watch as she whispers into his ear. From deep inside his throat rises a tuba-like shout. She is talking to him. They are having a conversation.

I feel obscene, standing there, as if I have witnessed the X-rated.

I decide to break up this little tea party and stumble toward them, yelling, "Sonora! Get off there!" She puts up a hand to ward me off and I grab it. One yank does the trick. I pull her down by me and wish for *his* death, my stomach tightening into something like jealousy.

"The hell were you thinking," I say and immediately fall victim to her eyeballs, crawling into me like a surgeon's knife, unpeeling my skin, boring open my pipework, unpacking enough muscle from my skeleton to fill a wheelbarrow. With her eyes, her beautiful eyes, she tears away my layers and makes me naked. From the basket of my ribcage she tugs a heart—a tiny thing, broken and hiccupping a beat. Unimpressed by its efforts she crushes it beneath her foot and it gets dirty. A smile crosses her face, greedy with understanding. She knows me in a special way—beyond all my brawn and horsemen bluster—and in a wave of desperation I squeeze her arms so hard there will no doubt be bruises come morning. She screams at me, a nonsense scream, and I scream back and smell the Coors puffing on my breath: "What in the goddamn hell are you doing out here, Sonora?"

She bites at me and I shake her body until it becomes an empty skin, ragdolled by my shakes. Faraway I hear a voice that must be mine, though I hardly recognize it: "You don't talk, Sonora. That's not your way. What were you telling, Mangold? Why won't you talk to me? Talk to *me*."

Mangold moves in with the hoof. It catches me below the knee and charlies the muscle into screaming knots. I stumble back, dragging both my leg and Sonora.

Mangold has his crown lowered, sharpened into white points from rubbing against fenceposts. I try to be the hero. I swing my fist and yell, "Get away from us, you goddamned monster." I wish myself strong but only feel jealous of his animal strength.

Then Mangold's ribs grow fat with air, the fuel to a roar. He charges two steps forward and unhinges his jaw—thundering out a scream wreathed in steam, so *deep* I hold up my hands to ward away the sound. You would have thought a cannon went off: the concussion echoes into my body and my blood ripples like when a stone is tossed into pondwater.

Mangold stamps his hooves and shakes his antlers and smoke tusks from his nostrils and I try to hide behind my beard while wishing for a gun to grip, a bullet to chamber, dreaming red punctures into his silver hide. He rises up on his haunches, hoofing the air.

Then Willow saves us? I am a blur of beer and adrenaline and hardly know up from down but somehow we end up outside the corral. Willow has Sonora in her arms and I am struck by how white her nightgown looks against her nut-brown skin. I paw at her, I say something lecherous, and like a good woman, she slaps me.

I wake up on the ground, salt in my joints, my eyelashes crusted together with frozen tears. While I slept a light rain fell and now the world is dewy with its after-breath. Clouds still hang here and there, light gray puffs that reach toward the ground. Small whips of lightning flash between them when I retrieve my revolver from the barn and march toward the corral, a sensation I associate with revisiting a crime scene.

Mangold's profile is gray in the light. He rests his chin on the fence, staring at the dark forest, no doubt dreaming his way into it, perhaps struggling through the trees, sipping water from a milky glacial stream.

I can't prove he feels and thinks and dreams, like us, but I believe it. His eyes regard me with hunger or thankfulness or fear—I don't know—when I swing open the gate and bow deep and say, "Get lost, your majesty."

He takes a few steps toward me, raising his antlered head like a king. When he huffs, the sound his breath makes rising up his throat makes me feel as if I am playing a dangerous game of chicken with one of those old steam engines.

He considers the gate, like: you're joking? Like he doesn't want to bother because I am just going to slam it in his face for a laugh. Or maybe he hesitates because he is afraid.

"You ought to be afraid," I say, my voice dank with drink and exhaustion.

He takes a few more cautious steps, jerking his head as if threatening to rake me aside—so I draw my revolver and *now* the feeling is mutual.

The first shot I aim at a moonlit cloud that looks like a cheerful Disney creature. It flares with lightning as if set afire by the bullet. Mangold tenses and lowers his horns, the muscles jumping beneath his hide.

The second shot blasts the dirt between us and he jumps and kicks at nothing and then goes galloping through the gate and across the meadow and into the woods, lost.

"God!" the man says. "This is truly God's country, ain't it?" His mouth lingers on the word "ain't" as if its taste is unfamiliar. He sighs and his breath smells of feet. He drives a silver BMW and he wears a gold necklace and a diamond earring. I have never understood jewelried men. He puts out a hand and it disappears inside mine. I give this one an extra squeeze along with my howdy. "My name's Francis," he says. Francis is a woman's name but I keep my quiet and tour him around the ranch.

Thanks, Francis. Thanks for the 5,000 bucks. Thanks and don't forget to point the gun away from your body. Don't forget to calibrate your shot with respect to wind and angle. Don't forget to wipe your ass.

I bleed these pantywaists for all they're worth—still providing the cowboy treatment so they don't suspect vampirism. Howdy, backslap, some weather we're having, bang! Good job, boys. Welcome to Foder Ranch, a place where the letting of blood makes you stronger, more alive.

I watch Sonora watching the wall. I don't speak but try to be the good father, standing in the doorway as if to say: I'm *here* for you. The other night clings to me. Even though she never said a word, a sort of conversation took place between us. I remember her staring through me, inside of me. Never have I felt more intimate with her, and the feeling remains barnacled to my mind. I can't forget it, feeling for once like we were communicating, like I had a real life daughter.

Outside Mangold is loose somewhere, ripping through the trees with his giant antlers, free. And maybe I'm a little jealous when I think of him reunited with his family, his animal friends. I imagine him claiming his forest throne while elk and other creatures dance around a bonfire like a bunch of savages, each taking turns licking his horns, all sticky with sap from sharpening against trees.

Sonora's back is rigid in her staring. I put a Patsy Cline tape in the stereo. Instead of snapping her fingers Sonora slaps her face and shakes her head and turns it off. Merle Haggard? Nope. I try Williams and Cash and Tillis and Parton but she won't listen to a word.

Come *on*, Sonora.

She unplugs the stereo and gets down on all fours and puffs up her chest and bugles—from the thin reed of her throat—the language of elk. It is like a native tongue—wild and startling—somehow more natural on her lips than if she said to me, "How do you do?" The windows tremble and threaten to shatter, along with my ears. I step back until the wall prevents any further escape.

Autism means wrong in the head. Autism means withdrawal into fantasy and Sonora, I figure, works like how my clients work. They come out here, their heart having pumped a lifetime of diet cola—and they want whiskey. They're tired. They've been made small and dickless by their wives and bosses and here they find a remedy, through the muzzle of a gun. Though the muzzle of a gun everything is under their control, everything makes perfect sense. Bang, I am powerful. Bang, I make a difference. *Bang*, we're all just meat in the shadow of the Cascade Mountains. Forget my sports car and 401K, family and civilization, prescription drugs. Here, among the mountains and beasts, the land breathes something raw. For a weekend, they rediscover some primal organ, they live a different sort of life—as seen through the hunter's scope, a faraway projection brought close, a fantasy made real.

They're all autistics. Maybe we're all a bunch of goddamn autistics.

Sonora lives in neverland. She used to dream her way through the sad soundtracks of country crooners but now honkytonk doesn't seem to suit her. She has instead found a hankering for the elk and their strange music. It is a terrible hankering. Just as her face is a terrible face—though beautiful—stark and open and obviously wanting nothing to do with me.

I say, "I'm here, Sonora." Mangold is not.

But it's him she wants. I know this because when I go to give her a hug she slaps the floor and shows her teeth and sings in a language I don't understand.

At breakfast—Spanish omelets drowned in salsa—I overhear Francis talking to my wife. He says, "What's your name, honey?" She tells him and he says, "I like your name. It makes me think of a creek bed and weeping willows draped over the creek." What a poet. He's just so happy to be here. He shakes his head and laughs and touches her on the elbow. "It's a real pretty name, Willow, because it paints a pretty picture to go along with your pretty face."

I wonder if Francis would like a rifle shoved up his butt.

After chow, I take my clients to the butcher parlor, to shark them into a sort of frenzy. They stare at the red curtains of meat, the pickled brains in jars like some carnival strangeness, a hog head on a hook. I say, "Go ahead and touch. It's all right to touch."

In here, the air smells like a bullet tastes. In here, blood drips from every corner. Just like that, one of the hunters faints, his head striking the concrete floor with a dull thud. All of us gather around and wait for him to wake up, and when he doesn't, I slap his cheek firmly enough to leave a red mark.

His eyes snap open and a minute later he's laughing, saying, "It's the altitude. It's altitude sickness. It's happened before." He complains of a headache and goes to get an Aspirin, but instead of returning to us, he hurries his bags into his car—one of those Lexus SUVs you could feed a trailer park with for a year—and slams the door. Gravel kicks up behind his wheels as he follows his shadow back to Portland.

The rest of the clients get a kick out this. They shove each other around like old pals and Francis says, "Man, what a pussy." A little after 7:00, they set off across the meadow, into the woods, wearing their ironed safari pants with the Velcro compartments and all sorts of zippers and buttons and hooks for hanging knives and compasses.

Where the trees meet the meadow, Francis turns and shows me the palm of his hand like an Indian chief. I copy the gesture and wish him good luck and he drops his hand and the woods swallow him up.

Three hours later a scream fills my head like an explosion of light.

I turn from the corral—empty except for the hoof prints pockmarking the drying mud—to see none other than Francis running toward me. The closer he gets, the worse he looks, his face all bloody with bits of forest stuck to it, his eyes wild and big enough so I can see their color, a liver green.

I take the pipe from my mouth and say, "What the hell got you?"

He says, "The biggest elk in the whole world!"

Mangold.

I ask for the story and he tells it: in a clearing of meadow, a rut-battle raged between some young bull and Mangold. When one of his grand antlers snapped, his head went lopsided with the weight. The other elk gored him along his flanks, his chest, until the fur shaved away and you could see his ribs. Mangold folded his legs and crumpled into a submissive pose, his heart pumping the life right out of him. The young bull snorted his victory and crashed off into the woods.

Francis figured he ought to go for the mercy kill. He aimed down the line of his rifle and cracked off a shot and made a rose of Mangold's neck.

But Mangold decided not to die. He pulled himself up, a nightmarish creature with blood siphoning fast from all his holes, and raced toward Francis.

Hearing the story I have visions of his sudden death—ribboned to pieces, stomped into burger—but no. Like an idiot he turned and ran directly into a tree, which opened up his forehead and hurt like a mother, but he kept on, afraid to look back, positive something dark and sharp-toothed chased him every inch of the way.

I know this because he tells me this, more or less. The rest I read in his expression. A terrified expression I have seen before, in the mirror, where I have spent many a drunk minute looking for virtues and finding few.

"So what should we do?" he says.

His face is a bizarre mix of colors: from greenish yellow to purple to red to black and everything in between. The branch tore him up good. It looks as if he has grown a second mouth just below his hairline. I think about the scar he will wear forever, forever thinking about me in front of the mirror, tracing the gummy white tissue with his finger.

When he blinks, tiny ruby tears race down his cheeks, along his neck, on toward his gold necklace, now red and looking like some kind of outside tendon. "So what should we do?" He is an emotional guy, a pathetic guy, but in a really weird way, I am starting to like him.

I say, "There's nothing to do except get you washed up."

A great bunch of noise interrupts that plan. Off in

the forest branches snap, pine needles sizzle, hooves thud against the hard-packed dirt. From Francis's hands I snatch his Remington, tug the bolt, chamber another round, just as Mangold emerges from the trees. He pauses, some twenty yards away, eyeing me.

Then a bad fit of coughing makes his whole body shake, and his head droops until it nearly touches the ground, as if following a scent there. A bloody oyster drools off his tongue and dampens the soil between his hooves.

I watch him through the scope, and when I see how his legs tremble under his weight, when I see he is no danger to us, I keep the pressure off the trigger. Through the scope everything is so close—the black pigment of his eyeball, each spike of hair, the green shoot of vein twisting along his ribcage—and under such scrutiny I feel like I know him, better now than in our ten years of company. He wants his corral, the safety and food and love that come with it. I understand completely.

His ribs bleed like crazy and scabs try to gum up the mess. Not ten paces away he stops and stares at me—right through the tunnel of the scope—and I feel the gears in my throat working as I swallow down a nugget of sadness. I motion with the rifle, toward the corral. "Go on," I say with my pipe clenched between my teeth. "Get back in there. Get back where you belong."

He raises a hoof and puts it down again. And then, as if some invisible string has been cut, he collapses into a bag of bones and a flock of swallows swirls from the forest, over the salt-grass meadow, dappling us with shadows.

As if on cue, a great bugling blooms from the forest, the sort of sound a big bunch of brontosauruses might make.

Behind me I hear laughter. I lower my rifle and shade my eyes and look toward the cabin and see Sonora framed by a window. She does not notice me, her eyes and ears focused on the forest. A look of joy creeps across her face and she giggles—a high-pitched tinkling that reminds me of wind chimes—and I know she is not without the capacity for love. She juts her lips and sings along with the animals and I want to comb her hair with my fingers, I want to pepper her face with kisses, I want her to blow me a kiss, wave, acknowledge me in *some* way.

But just like these woods, she is out of my control.

My pipe is dead and I tap the bowl in my palm and scatter the remaining ashes over Mangold. And then, in a flood of emotion, I puff up my chest and sing along with the elk. Sounds boom between my lips. At first I sing just to hear my throat, to remind me I'm alive. Then I feel a shifting inside, like some worm turning over in its sleep, and a warm sensation plays across my skin like a Chinook breeze. I begin to feel strong—sort of the way shooting makes me feel—and we all sing together and the sound, the purest sound you can imagine, rises up and fills the world and eventually fades.

The Colony

We like it here. We never want to leave. Not ever. I'm talking about the 300 acres Seb Holmes bought at auction for a song. He sold chunks of it, and because I had some money, and because I knew Seb, I bought a pretty big chunk, thirty acres. I can walk an hour and not leave my land. Not many people can say that. Not many people understand what you can do with this kind of space.

All around us are the Cascade Mountains, bearded with old-growth forests—mainly Douglas firs, some spruce and alder, cottonwood—that give way at higher elevations to huckleberry and manzanita and beyond that, lichen and glaciers and rock. This is a twenty-minute drive from Portland, if you can believe it. Twenty minutes and you're in the middle of nowhere.

All together there are ten of us. And we are not just anybodies. We were *chosen* by Seb to serve a certain function. We have a mechanic. We have an accountant. We have a chef—and man, can he cook. We have a doctor and a dentist and a pastor. We have an agriculturist. We *have* to have an agriculturist—Seb says—partly for the food we grow—the sweet corn and the yellow onions and the Irish potatoes, the red delicious apples that taste as good as they sound—but mainly for the weed.

We have so much weed, you have no idea. We smoke it and we sell it, and we sell it by slipping the buds into the hollowed-out Gideon Bibles that Pastor

Bart hauls downtown in his VW van, setting up shop on a street corner, proselytizing. He grows his beard long and speaks of eternal damnation with enough brimstone to keep your everyday citizens at a distance. When a paying customer picks up a Bible and drops a hundred-dollar bill in the offering pot, Pastor Bart winks and says, "God bless you."

Anyway, whatever money we make selling weed—which is plenty—goes into a communal bank account we use for fertilizer, for ammunition, for electricity, for food, for beer, for tools, for toys and parties. We are a community—a colony, Seb calls it—and if we didn't have to work jobs, buy groceries, punch numbers into the ATM, we wouldn't.

I live in a big two-story cabin with a red steel roof. Just me. Which is great, if not a little lonely. Seb designed it. He designed all our cabins. He is an architect and contractor who sketches blueprints for those houses you sees in subdivisions, the ones that look like they came from a box. How we met is I'm the guy who builds those houses that look like they came from a box.

Back then, when we first met, if you get right down to it, I didn't amount to much. I spent my days striking things with hammers, my nights drinking deeply and profoundly toward a dreamless sleep, fighting. There was this bar I used to visit, called the Someplace Else Tavern, where the floor was ankle-deep with sawdust and there was a tooth, a human tooth, imbedded in the bar. Everybody had a different story about how the tooth got there.

But I *knew*.

I am the one who slammed the guy—the guy with the bandito mustache and the attitude—into the counter with such force that when he pulled his face away, the tooth remained, its roots gleaming red.

Back in the heydays I would carry electrical tape in my back pocket and around midnight, if a fight hadn't found me, I would wrap my knuckles and find a fight. At the time, even though I couldn't imagine what else I might do with myself, I fell into a convict's funk, looking forward and seeing only a life-sentence, all double bourbons and warm lumber and hydraulic oil.

Seb changed all that. Seb *changed* me.

One night after a hard day banging together some subdivision—Moose Cock Heights or whatever—he and I shared a hitter out behind the dumpster behind the tavern. All around us rats licked at broken eggshells and scurried through crumpled newspaper, when Seb said, "This might seem like a strange question, but are you happy? And when I say happy, I mean *happy*."

The rest is history.

Seb is a planner and a talker and maybe a genius, and I am none of these things. He can talk for hours about some planet or philosopher you never heard of, and sometimes he does.

He wears a beard that screams I-just-came-out-of-the-woods!

The thing about Seb is, he's short. The lifts in his boots barely elevate him above the status of dwarf. I'm talking *short*. And I have to admit, the straightness of his spine, his vertical-striped shirts, his loud voice, his untamed beard, make me wonder if he isn't compensating for something. Like maybe this colony is one big compensation.

Take our cabins for instance. They're huge—as huge as Seb is small. In my living room I could stick a thirty-foot Christmas tree, all lit up with powdery lights, if I wanted. When I said, "Do I really need a place this big," Seb said, "Yes, you do. That's exactly what you need." And it was.

Sometimes I race through the cabin, naked, except for my wool socks, sliding along the wideboard floors, with the lights blazing, with the stereo blaring, for the sense of freedom. And sometimes I take my pistol—a Hardballer .45 Seb got me for my 30th—and blast holes in the walls and ceiling, howling. Just because.

Together we built the cabin. Tractors growled around, uprooting trees, pushing dirt with their broad metal shovels, clearing a space for the cement truck to lay the foundation upon which we stacked logs straight as a plumb line, caulked tight to choke away the wind. Chainsaws snarled and sandpaper hissed and hammers cracked like some mechanical storm.

When it was finally finished, I took a deep breath to take in the cabin, the forest, the colony, and my part in it, along with the smell of sap, which you could smell all the way at Seb's place, some five miles distant, when the wind got going good.

And when I exhaled, I tasted the bong-water vinegar of my life before Seb, of two o'clock in the morning last calls and stumbling home with a broken nose.

We throw parties. And when we throw them, we throw them. Imagine a hundred drunks milling around ten pigs roasting on spits. Imagine kegs of Black Butte Porter. Imagine buckets of steaming chili, platters of pickled trout fingerlings, caramel cake and peach pie and a hookah pipe packed with the finest greenery you'll ever encounter. Imagine a hundred yards of extension cables snaking from my cabin to the woods so we might watch big-screen baseball under the stars. Imagine an amphitheater dug from the side of a hill with the Portland Shakespeare Company performing Shakespeare, the Portland Pops Symphony Orchestra performing German composers I can't pronounce.

Imagine a trebuchet the size of a sailboat. I'm talking a fifteen-foot arm. I'm talking a sixty-pound counterweight. I'm talking about hurling large stones, dead marmots, pumpkins, watermelons, and even milk jugs full of flaming gasoline maybe, like, say, two hundred feet or so. I'm talking about serious fun.

You can have a hundred drunks at a party and they will go dead quiet when they see that milk jug soaring above their heads, letting off this spectral light, pinkish, greenish, and when it lands, it detonates. I'm talking a flaming mushroom the size of a small house. It is nothing less than beautiful.

Just imagine.

Surrounded by a meadow surrounded by firs, Seb's porch, like my porch, like all the other porches here at the colony, is the nice wraparound kind with homemade rockers—made from larch and stained with teak oil and sealed with shellac—set on either side of the front door.

Twilight, I go here to rock and talk and drink and

smoke, to watch the horizon go crazy with color. Seems like every moth in the county flaps around our heads, their papery wings stirring the air. They are Pandora moths, mainly, big ones, as big as an open hand. The porch light draws them. Sometimes they land on our heads and shoulders and laps, to rest, and sometimes they land on our beer bottles, to taste.

There is a hookah set between us and Seb takes a deep hit from it. Words smoke from his mouth and I follow the smoke until it gets lost in the purpling haze when he says, "I want to ask you a question. Because you're a man, you know about things, right?"

I say shoot. He makes his hand into a gun and goes *coo*.

Then he says, "All my life, I've felt dissatisfied with *where* I am." For such a little guy, he's got a deep voice, a professor's voice. It surprises people. It enchants them. "You know, like there was some mix-up in the space-time continuum or whatever. Like this moment wasn't my moment. You ever feel that way?"

"All the time," I say.

He winks or else has something in his eye. "Where would you be? If you could choose *any*where, *any*time, to be, where would you be?"

The answer lies in the hookah. I draw smoke deep into my lungs and feel my wrist veins constrict. I smack my mouth with the skunky sweet flavor. Inspiration swirls behind my eyeballs. "Sometimes I have this dream where I wake up and I'm the only person left. There are empty cars in the middle of the highway. There are casseroles rotting on supper tables. There are tigers and wolves roaming through the streets. It's like the rapture happened or something. Anyway, I walk around and explore all the abandoned streets and houses and grocery stores and I do whatever the hell I please. Go naked. Burn money. Hunt animals in department stores. Anything."

Smoke leaks from his nose when he says, "For real?"

I say, "For real what?"

"For-real-you-dream-that for real?"

"Yeah, I dream that."

He shakes his head and a smile creeps up his cheeks. "You're a good man, Charlie Brown." He puts out his hand and I grasp it and shake it in the arm-wrestling way, and when we release our grip, I have to admit a part of me is disappointed, a part of me wants to keep on holding him.

A moth lights on my forehead and flexes its wings and I don't brush it away.

I ask Seb what about him—if he could be anywhere, where would he be, and he says, "I would be right here." He points to the porch for emphasis. "Only rewind a century or so. Transferred to a time when you could shoot someone who did you wrong and that would be okay." A small pink tongue darts out and licks his lips, hungry for the dream. "I like to think I'd do all right. Quick draw, talented horseman, resilient drinker, feared by men and cherished by women, you know?"

I knew.

"Wild West times," he says, his voice all soft and wistful. "But you know what? We can't complain. We've got it really good here. This is the life. *The* life."

I agree and I mean it—and when night comes on in earnest, despite the glow of Portland, we can make out the stars, foggy and distant, like coins at the bottom of a dirty fountain.

This warm June afternoon we're at the Wal-Mart Supercenter, picking up supplies, when a man in a crushed-velvet leisure suit points at the ceiling and yells, "There's a vulture." And he's right, there is. Maybe it was attracted to the smell of the butchery or maybe it chased a rat through the electric sliding doors or maybe it caught a bad air current—I don't know—but there it is, flapping among the white metal rafters, squawking and casting pinfeathers to the air-conditioned air like seeds that lazily float down to the floor, the floor mopped to a linoleum glow.

We follow its flight, shoving our way past the human traffic, the Neanderthals and Wildabeasts who shuffle along in sweatpants, smelling like Spaghetti-Os, concentrating on their coupons.

The vulture circles Hardware and lands in Electronics, in the middle of the aisle. One of those How-Can-I-Help-You zombies in a blue vest chucks a DVD at it, and it hisses, opening its wings as if in greeting. It cocks its bald red head, observing us with its bird eye, and then with one heavy flap of its wings lifts itself into the air, sailing over to Groceries.

We follow it there.

It tries to roost on some top-shelf cereal boxes, unsuccessfully, knocking them to the floor, along with jars filled with pickled beets that splatter across the aisle, so red. Next is the butchery, where, perhaps frenzied by the smell of blood, the vulture drops down to skitter across the stainless steel counter, its claws clicking, trying to find purchase. A butcher—a woman butcher, a butcheress—she screams in her bloody apron and so does the bird and so does Seb when he withdraws the 9mm Glock from inside his coat.

Holy shit is what I'm thinking.

The pistol jumps, the explosion so loud it blows every other sound from the store, leaving behind a scary silence Muzak and the shrieks of women will soon take over. The buzzard does a little dance and falls over, missing most of its left side and leaking all over the place.

"Let's get out of here," Seb says and I say, "Yeah. Let's."

On our way back to the colony Seb whistles as if nothing happened, as if I'm not checking the rearview every five seconds for flashing lights.

Today is a bright blue day and everything and everyone looks bleached of its color under the sun.

Seb digs around beneath his seat, removing a silver cigarette case he thumbs open to reveal six big blunts, so meticulously rolled they're like their own kind of art. He lights one and the flame releases its sweet damp-hay smell. He takes a mean drag and with the smoke boiling in his lungs swings a last-minute right into a new subdivision to check out this fountain-in-the-middle-of-the-driveway schema he wants to incorporate into his next proposal. He steadily releases the smoke downward, where it spreads across his lap. "You know," he says, rocketing over a speed bump, swiveling his head side to side to inspect the carefully trimmed hedges, the billiard-table lawns, the gray plastic siding and bone-white shutters and river-rock chimneys. "This place would almost be pretty, if it wasn't so damn ugly."

A week ago, things changed between us.

Seb shows up with this girl, Janet. Got homeless written all over her. Says she's twenty-five but I'm thinking teenager. Says she needs a place to stay, to get her bearings, a couple hot meals and a couple hot showers.

I practically shit.

There is a homeless situation in Portland. Downtown, along the Willamette River, in Pioneer Courthouse Square, you'll see them. They're the ones squatting on the street vents, for the warmth, reading crumpled paperbacks, playing strange whistles, asking for change to call their mother. They wear a special type of clothes that reminds me of the really, really old ham sandwich you'll find in the back corner of your fridge, sort of wrinkly and kind of slimy and pretty much something you don't want to touch except pinched between your forefinger and thumb on its way to the garbage.

When Seb goes downtown, he goes nuts. Some guy with duct tape on his shoes asks for a buck, Seb gives him twenty. He does this frequently enough they know him by face. We can't go anywhere without getting swarmed. You should see the way he hands out money, *our* weed money, big greasy clumps of bills, as if to rid him of the weight.

I don't get Seb sometimes. Sometimes he seems so brilliant, like he has this special plan for us. A vision.

Then he goes and throws away our weed money, money he says is meant to build a community.

Now this. Now he brings to us the very problems we're here to escape. Now he comes home with a stray dog answers by the name of Janet, always looking at him like she's looking for a belly rub.

Here is what happens when Seb introduces us: she puts out her hand for a shake, and I let it hang there.

"You're kidding me," I say, conscious of a sort of watery anger filling me up, so I can barely breathe, so I can smell sawdust and see a tooth embedded in a bar counter.

"I am not kidding you," he says.

"You're shitting me," I say.

"I am not shitting you," he says.

I sense my expression tightening. Janet smiles in a lifeless way and gives up on the handshake, taking a step back, studying her sandals, as if wondering who made them.

There is something hooded in my voice when I say, "Unbelievable," something dark with red lines running through it, and then I turn and walk away from them.

Of course I later apologize. This is at Seb's cabin, where bear traps and fishing rods and crisscrossed snowshoes and rusted metal placards advertising Red Rock Cola decorate the walls. Seb sits on his leather couch with one hand resting in his crotch. This makes him feel stronger. He looks at me like he looked at the vulture, his eyes narrowed, his lips pinched into a white anus. "I'm only going to tell you this once," he says, amping up the baritone for the professorly effect. “Don’t ever talk to me like that again. I won’t tolerate it.”

We, who have shared so much, have arrived at this, growling and posturing over a goddamn girl. “My bad,” I say, my voice whining a touch.

He stares at me and I look away, because the worst thing you can do is look a biting dog in the eye. He snaps his fingers to get my attention—says, “Hey,”—and gives me the Plains Indian hand signal for don’t-sweat-it-bro. “We’re all here to let real life go,” he says, “to escape.” He combs his beard with his fingers. “Here we got someone, just a girl, who’s been dealt a bad hand, the chips stacked against her. I would think you of all people could dig giving her a taste of freedom.”

There is, he thinks, hope for improving her—like me.

He says, “Just for a little bit, yeah?”

“Yeah,” I say. “Cool.” I mean, whatever. But my wide teeth-showing smile is enough to convince Seb everything is settled, and so he rises from the couch and slow-motion slugs my shoulder and a minute later we’re outside shooting arrows into human silhouettes, the firing-range kind, taped to trees.

Janet smells like campfires. She has a wide, almost square, sort of masculine face. She has a way of chomping her gum, of drinking straight from the whiskey bottle, of sitting slouched down with her legs wide open. It’s enough to make me imagine pressing against her in a tavern somewhere, looking for an excuse to stroke her arm, lean in for a kiss, tell her lies about my life, invite her home to hammer the headboard, to buck her pelvis against mine.

Don't get me wrong: I don't like the girl.

Though I pretend to, because Seb wants me to. I don't know. There is something about her that reminds me of me—the old me—her bearing and her attraction to Seb. When we are together, drinking and eating, I feel an ache spreading inside me—an ache like your knuckles experience when striking someone in the mouth—at first dull and warm, intensifying into an arterial throb.

And as for Seb, there is something new about him, his demeanor, something I don't recognize. We used to be close like the men from Western movies, cracking belly laughs around a campfire, slugging each other affectionately, but now, not so much. There is something between us—a rift—goes by the name Janet.

"Look at all the stars," she says. "I never knew there were so many stars."

"Man, did you ever smell air that smelled this great?" she says, whistling a breath through her nose. "It smells like Christmas."

She has one of those sick voices. You know, a little scratchy, throaty, like pebbles rattling around in a cardboard tube. She has black hair down to her butt and always fusses with it, braiding it, combing it, sometimes even chewing it, if she's preoccupied.

I wonder what it tastes like.

"You have it so good here," she says. "Don't ever leave this place."

I tell her she can count on that.

No matter what our differences, gasoline brings us together, here at the colony, as a relatively cheap and relatively safe form of entertainment.

Listen to me when I say *relatively* safe.

When it is cold is when gasoline is dangerous. The fumes stay low and spread like lard melting in a pan. Once Seb lit a couch soaked, just drenched, in gasoline in the middle of December. You should have seen it! He sparks a match and a blue pancake—two feet tall and twenty feet wide—appeared.

Foomp. Just like that. A wreath of heat knocking me a step or two in reverse, knocking Seb back on his back. One second there's snow covering the ground—the next second, *gone*—replaced by a big muddy oval boiling and snapping with blue fire.

Lucky for Seb, I yanked him out of all that blueness. Lucky for Seb, he was wearing coveralls, Carhartt coveralls, made from the most resilient material on earth next to titanium and diamonds. Had it not been for the coveralls, forget about it. As is, his boots and gloves melted, his eyelashes charred, his hair smoldered, and for about a week his face glowed an unhealthy red, as if all his blood had been brought to it.

Now, on the porch, when Seb tells Janet the gasoline story, she nods and maintains eye contact even as she goes to town on the hookah. This is her fifth hit and this is premium bud. I'm talking THC up the wazoo. She takes a muscular draw and the hookah emits a gurgling sound. Her lungs and then her cheeks fill with smoke, her eyes go glassy, and she sort of leans, sort of swoons against Seb's rocker, giggling.

Seb doesn't seem to notice. He, too, is blazed out of his mind and on top of that caught up in his story, as if reliving it, as if hypnotized by the sound of his own voice. He moves his hands like he does when talking, like pale moths flapping around his head and into his lap where they wrestle before reaching out to stroke Janet's thigh.

Seeing this reminds me of the conversation we had a couple days ago, when fishing for brook trout. "She is so, so, so good in bed," he said, slipping a leech on his hook. "I mean: wow." Black goop dribbled down his palm and he wiped it on his thigh and plopped the leech in the water. "I mean: holy shit. I mean: do yourself a favor and go out and get yourself a girl. And I mean pronto. Your life could stand some improvement."

About then and about now I could have gone for another beer.

It's hard, seeing them together. It's like seeing your father drunk or your mother dating another man. It's like seeing your friend have an orgasm or a seizure. It's like an altered condition you're not comfortable with.

Seb finishes the gasoline story like he always finishes the gasoline story. "And man, my face was burned so bad it was like this beet, man, this big red fucking beet."

Janet says, "Poor baby," and touches his cheek. "Will you show me? Will you burn something? Right now? For me?"

I jump from my rocker and say in a too loud voice, "I'll go get some fuel!"

We have this car, this old Oldsmobile, and though springs poke through its upholstery and though its brakes chirp and its engine groans, it is a good reliable car we use to ramble around the colony. We shoot it, occasionally, but not to hurt. We shoot it for aesthetic reasons.

Now it is parked before Seb's cabin and I place on its hood a plastic bucket full of gasoline. "Give us the foomp," Seb says. "We want to hear the foomp."

"Yeah," Janet says and cuddles down into Seb's lap. "Foomp."

I fire a match and deliver the foomp. Flames rise from the bucket and Seb applauds and Janet hoo-rahs and the gasoline burns this ghostly blue color, making the Oldsmobile look like some otherworldly police vehicle. Which is cool, for all of thirty seconds. Then the bucket begins to buckle and melt and all at once something gives.

There is a hissing sound when the flames spread across the hood, looking like the purest water—so impossibly blue—waterfalling down the grill, crackling the paint into black curls, seeping into the engine where things sizzle and pop. The sight is strangely beautiful, and I just stand there with my head cocked, watching.

Seb wakes me from my daze with a "She's gonna blow!" and we run inside, all three of us stoned and laughing so hard we cry. "Oh, Jesus," Seb says, "I'm going to bust a gut." We peek out the window, saying shit, shit, *shit*, but the car never blows—the front tires burst and the engine is toast—but that's it, no ka-boom, and maybe we are more than a little disappointed.

Our agriculturist, K.B. Woodrell—whose eyes are bloodshot, whose fingernails are rimmed with dirt—

says we have too many males. And though at first I think he is talking about something else, he is talking about weed.

Our horticulture takes place largely in the bear-grass meadows, of which there are many. We grow Indica and Sativa strains, and hybrids, the kind of thick beautiful buds you've only seen on the Nightly News with Tom Brokaw. To fend off the deer we circle each plant with blood and hair, mainly raccoon, some possum, whatever ends up trapped in the many steel-mesh cages stationed around the colony.

We intersperse the weed with sticker bushes and dwarf pines because sometimes the black helicopters buzz all up and down our woods, giant lawnmowers of the heavens. Men in bulletproof vests hang out the open doors with binoculars and infrared cameras pressed to their eyes. We wave at them. They get waved at. We know what they're looking for, and they won't find it.

We plant every plant to the east side of a disguising bush or tree, because weed needs at least five hours of direct sunlight a day, and for some reason it takes easier to the morning rays. And "because the feds typically work in north-south search patterns," K.B. says, his mouth cocked in a lazy smile. "They're weird like that. Something about shadows."

As an extra precaution K.B. trims the herb and ties it to the ground and affectionately calls it Herb Junior. "And though Herb Junior's bud yield is not as hot as it could be," K.B. says, "Herb Junior does what he can."

K.B. knows his dope. He spends his days fertilizing, weeding, watering, testing ph levels, adding peat moss to make the soil more porous. And when we throw parties, when everyone passes around the old peace pipe, K.B. crawls around, collecting our spilled seeds into a plastic Ziploc baggie. He says, "Acquiring and maintaining a quality seed stock is the most fundamental task of a successful grower," and we say, "Okay, K.B. Whatever you say."

"Whatever you say, K.B.," is what we tell him when he tells us we have too many males.

"Eighty percent," he says and shakes head, like: man.

"This is bad?" Seb says.

"Hardly any females means hardly any harvest means hardly any cash means hardly any money means hardly any beer," K.B. says.

"This is bad," Seb says.

"You can say that again, bro," K.B. says.

About twice a month the colony gathers together for supper, as we do tonight, partly to discuss business, but mainly as an excuse to drink. Under the stars we sit at a big banquet table made from the wideboard leftovers of my cabin flooring. At its head sits Seb, like some strange poo-bah, wearing a football helmet with antlers attached to it. The antlers are set high and thrown back and big enough so that when he wears the helmet, it weighs his head down into his shoulders, so he appears to have no neck.

Normally I sit to his right—"My right-hand man," he calls me—but tonight Janet takes my spot. I find a place elsewhere, between K.B. and Pastor Bart, who click their steak knives together playfully and say, "En guard."

A bonfire crackles nearby, making shadows on our faces.

Our cook, Travis Junk—who wears sweatpants and a blue-jean jacket that can't hide his poochy belly—serves us venison steaks drowned in a hickory barbeque sauce, twice-cooked potatoes, and some sort of dope salad crumbled over with gorgonzola cheese. When everyone comments on how delicious it all tastes, I realize I'm not tasting anything, my eyes on Seb and Janet. They feed each other bites of food, and I notice Janet holds her fork like I hold my fork, like a gravy ladle.

And so we eat and we drink and we talk and eventually decide to have a hundred seeded females shipped up from Humboldt, California.

The pain in our muscles and the concern for the crop and the cold beer tasting so good, it all creates a rowdy appetite such as men get after working a hard job. We drink Black Butte Porter straight from the bottle, quickly, like pop. Our knives clatter against our plates and we soak up the leftover blood with great hunks of tangy sourdough. Our bellies swell over our belts and when there is nothing left to eat, we hack up a willow bush for sticks for roasting marshmallows.

Janet drinks like a pro. She drinks so much her teeth must be floating. At one point she takes my hand and leans against me and I feel her breath.

Seb runs an extension cable from his cabin and sets up his stereo system in the bear grass. From the speakers a dozen fiddles saw a fast jig and he pumps up the volume until you can *feel* it. He does a goofy little half-step with one hand wrapped around a whiskey bottle and the other hand on top his helmet as if to hold it there. Everybody claps to the beat. Janet takes one look at him and throws back her head and laughs her loud mannish laugh. Everybody loves that laugh. Everybody wants to hear it again. So one by one the men start in with their own goofy dance moves—K.B. doing a few Egyptian movements with his arms and head—while the rest of them stomp their feet, wave their hands, going *yoo-hoo*, trying to get her attention.

The men make a circle and Janet stands in its middle and claps and laughs when they swirl around and around her, each man's chest at the back of the next man, cheek to jowl, when they beat their feet into the grass, trampling it down.

This is Friday night and for the past five days they have been abused by their jobs, they have been like animals in a pen, and now they are drunk and excited and hungry. You can see it in their faces.

It's that old instinct.

I stand a short distance away and watch with my arms crossed, tapping my feet and smiling, awkwardly, at the strange picture that makes me want very badly to put Janet in a bag to hide someplace.

Seb breaks from the other men and shakes his antlers and paws at the ground, pretending he is a deer, sort of galloping to the banquet table, where earlier he placed his acoustic guitar. The men slow their dancing, as if the game is no longer fun without him.

Seb is always surprising you. Behind that mask of exaggerated folksiness is a guy who can sit down at a piano or pick up a flute and belt out Mozart one second,

Merle Haggard the next. He slips the guitar strap around his neck and with a pink pick strikes a few chords that tremble in the air. The men stop dancing and all our eyes observe him with a steady interest. He strikes another string or two and toys with the tuning pegs and Janet breaks through the men and shuts off the stereo. "Play," she says and picks up a beer bottle and holds it with two hands. "Would you please please please play?"

The men look at one another with something like embarrassment, and at Seb with something like resentful admiration, before retreating to where they left their beers.

Seb goes to town on the guitar with reckless abandon,his eyes closed, his fist tumbling up and down the strings, so he doesn't seem to play any one song in particular. Instead he plays what sounds like a whole bunch at once, letting his pick find its own way, real cool and rockabilly, while his elegant fingers march up and down the frets.

The men keep their eyes sharp on Janet, who makes a *woo* noise and says, "Lick that box, baby," and starts bending her knees and swirling in circles like an Indian fancydancer. Her black hair shakes and trembles, always a second behind her body. The men stare. They love her. They *want* her. And when all of them step forward, toward her, like moths drawn to flame, I step back—and onto the foot of another guy.

This is Bob. Bob is a dentist. He looks like a bullfrog in a polo shirt. "The fuck off me," he says and shoves me into the table. Its bench strikes my knees and my mouth puckers around the pain.

The guitar seems to grow louder, as if approaching something.

Bob has twenty pounds on me but I have fifty bar fights on Bob. About now I could use some electrical tape to wrap around my knuckles. I say, "You are in some deep hot water, friend," and stand up straight to underline the threat.

Seb plucks a fast series of high notes and I try to shove Bob but Bob resists and tosses me back into Pastor Bart, who says, "Jesus," and falls on Seth Anderson, a diesel mechanic with three teeth and nothing to lose. So it gets to be a big fight. There's a lot of punching. Bottles get broken. Seth picks up a plate and brings it down on Bob. Bob collapses and Pastor Bart stomps on his back before getting smacked in the nose by a jerked elbow.

I spot Janet slipping the antler helmet off Seb, putting it on her own head. She climbs up on the table and raises her hands, like a child imitating a flower, smiling. I push my way through the rout, moving toward them, toward her—I don't know why—but no matter where I step, there is something, a body, glass, beer or blood, something slippery that makes sucking sounds against my boots.

I slip and end up on top of Bob, who ends up on top of me. His knuckles batter my ribs and I short-punch him in the face, crushing his cheek. He lets out a braying sound and reaches for my neck. My breath gets hot and tight and he starts to look fuzzy and a long way off. Over his shoulder Janet appears, smiling, swinging a bottle like a Louisville slugger. There is a line-drive crack and Bob shivers a little and opens his mouth. It is like a basket to put pain into. He falls off me and leaves a burning necklace around my throat. I choke in a few breaths and Janet says, “Wow, I always wanted to do that.” In her eyes I see something friendly and at the same time fierce, an animal brownness.

A moth flutters between us and I say, “Thanks,”—meaning it and resenting it.

Seb’s guitar picking filters into the fight, a hillbilly riff, all hot whiskey and barbed wire. Listen: he is *into* his music. He is *feeling* it. He nods away, bending his knees, bending his body into a question mark, every sound like a burst of color that trembles down his spinal cord and makes him feel free or powerful or *un*domesticated or whatever.

Our eyes meet. His lips split open and some laughter spills out and gets mixed up with my nerves so I feel like some great twanging string he tickles with his finger. And with the men fighting all around us I can’t help but laugh, too, at what he has created, at the wildness of it all.

Seb is at a city council meeting, discussing zoning rights, when I bang on his cabin door. Janet opens up wearing cut-offs and a purple bikini top. From behind her comes the sound of the TV and something cooking: pork, I imagine, bubbling in salty black beans.

I take a stutter-step toward her and for a second don’t know what to say. I concentrate on her face so she won’t think I’m turned on by her breasts, her belly, the dark mole on her hip. She gives me a steady look, a daring look—like: you wish—and my shy interest in her body seems unclean, even dangerous.

“Yeah?” she says, her voice full of barroom gravel.

"What do you want?" She squares her shoulders as if ready to wrestle. "Hello? You here?"

I can hear the sound of my pulse in my ears. I hand her a backpack. "Here. You take this."

For a moment, before she takes the bag, her face creases with puzzlement, and I wonder can she smell the pot fumes puffing off it. "Just take it," I say. "Open it."

Her eyes bounce between me and what I'm handing her, watching for any mismove on my part, I assume. When she unzips the zipper, a big block of air flooded with that tea-leaves-brewed-in-cat-piss smell comes roaring out, making all oxygen within a five-foot radius seem scarce.

"That is A-1 world-class premium bud," I say. "Sensamilla. Eighty ounces. You know how much money that's worth?"

She shakes her head, *no*, looking at me under all that hair.

"A lot. Thousands. I'm figuring about seven thousand." I lift my hands into a palms-up gesture and say, "Smoke it, sell it, I don't give a damn, but take it. Okay? Just take it."

For a moment she's quiet, looking into the backpack, her nostrils flared. Then her eyes rise and meet mine and she says, "Look, I'm just fucking him. It's no big deal. You don't have to have a cow over it." She lifts one linebacker hand—calluses, gnawed fingernails—to her hair and twirls a curl around her finger.

"I don't believe you're with him for the long haul," I say. "I believe you're with him for the vacation, to escape whatever it is you're escaping."

That nudges her enough to say, "Yeah?"

"That backpack is overflowing with escape. No strings attached."

She shuts her mouth and purses her lips at a steady rhythm, like a fish. Her eyes squint, searching for an answer, and then she reaches into the pack as if to withdraw one, withdrawing instead a big nugget, so tight and resinous. She pops it in her mouth—just like that—and starts crunching away at it like a stubborn hunk of celery. That's like thirty dollars. That's like such a terrific waste of a dragonmaster of a smoke session. Even though the weed is hers, I can't help but twitch.

If I had that nugget inside me, if had a buzz behind my eyes, she would be easier to manage. She would be entertaining, the comedy smash of the summer, and I would be relaxed and unafraid. Being stoned, for me, is like standing in the middle of a big cornfield and howling—a great calming release.

Yes, if there is a *reason* for marijuana, I am it.

"You think about it," I say, and through a soggy green mouthful she says, "I will. Thanks for stopping by." In her neck a vein pulses slowly, and a big part of my unhappiness fades away when I lift my hand, waving good luck, goodbye.

Maybe we are not so different, Janet and I. Both with history, as they say, both orphans brought in from the cold, taken under Seb's wing, our lives turning on a dime as the greener grass arrived by the midnight train, so to speak.

But I can't, I *won't*, share.

With Seb, I have slashed the tires of a Mercedes with a bowie knife. With Seb, I have learned to call crows by fitting grass into the end of a split branch. With Seb, I have shot the bull, I have laughed, I have wept, I have given and received good-natured shit, which is what every man looks for in a buddy.

With Seb, I have sliced holes in a Sealy posturepedic mattress—into which we stuffed ammunition, every kind of bullet you can imagine—and drenched the thing in gasoline and launched it into the river that snakes through the colony, the Sandy River, its waters milky white from glacial till. We dropped a match and the fire took to the mattress in a great snapping coil that floated away from us like one of those ceremonial Viking grave things, flaming, exploding.

With Seb I have blazed through a blunt and pretended to be a Mohican warrior. Picture us leaping over logs and ducking under branches, giggling, hunting jackrabbits and coveys of quail with potato guns, me turning my head every few steps to make sure he was still there.

Made from PVC pipe and ignited by hairspray, the potato gun makes a very loud bang when it launches its payload the length of a football field or through a particleboard target, or through a quail, leaving behind feathers and not much else.

The other day Seb showed Janet how to use them. *Our* potato guns! He snuggled up behind her, as you would when teaching someone how to golf, and together they tapped the lantern lighter. The five-foot cannon jumped in their arms, the spud rocketing into the distance, knuckling, wobbling, as if uncertain of its course.

It is dawn and it is muggy and it strikes me, now that Janet is gone, now that Seb sits next to me on the porch, wearing his antler helmet, teary and drunk after an all-night bender, how much I love this man. I *love* him, as a friend and a brother both, more deeply than you can imagine. When we are together, drinking and joking, I feel a warmth spreading inside me—a sense of belonging, of knowing it feels so right to be here, at the colony, with him.

We watch K.B. push a wheelbarrow through the meadow. In the morning light dew sparkles a purplish color. The wheelbarrow is crowded with female marijuana plants, seeded—some cross-pollinated strain that arrived yesterday by U-Haul, and K.B. has been working all night, to avoid detection, planting, to ensure a good crop for Pastor Bart to pawn, for the benefit of us all.

For the benefit of us all is exactly why *she* had to go.

I dig another couple beers from the cooler and we clink them together—"To Janet," we say—before drinking to mourn and to celebrate her departure.

Seb looks terrible, big bags under his eyes like he's been punched. He blows a sigh out his nose, all lackluster and making me make another toast, to see him smile. "To us," I say and it works, he smiles. Again we clink bottles and drink and he swishes the beer around in his mouth like mouthwash before swallowing it down. "Yeah," he says. "For sure. To us, man." There's a lotof exhale in his voice, its energy gone.

I wonder…if he had to make a choice, who would he pick? Her or me?

Any lingering anxiety vanishes when he says, "You know what? I'm thinking this is a good thing." He puts his hand on mine and leaves it there. His fingers move—so very slightly—reminding me of a heartbeat. "I'm thinking I'm happy about this."

I give him a hopeful smile and say, "Me too."

I am a fool for him, and I guess my selfish happiness,my relief, is the proof.

Behind us is Portland, the skyscrapers rising above the trees, glimmering in the half-light, looking like several dozen spaceships ready to launch to the moon. Before us are the Cascades. The sun crests the saddle between Mt. Hood and Jefferson, flaring, haloing the chain of mountains with a light red light that draws my eyes to the sky, the enormous blue sky, where high above us a vulture circles, fat off carcasses, its feathers shining greasy, able to see what we cannot.

The colony has changed, we have changed, and off toward Portland acres of clay and basalt and fir are being bulldozed to make way for yet another subdivision.

Bigfooting

I have been searching for years. I have seen the footprints, the rough reddish hair, the plum-sized piece of poop. I have heard his sad sweet cries rising from deep in the woods. Bigfoot exists. Believe me, believe it, and know that I am *this close* to proving it.

All I need is a body.

My wife of three years, Heidi, she is beginning to believe. At first she was all yeah right. We would argue six days to Sunday. Then I showed her the poop. She has since changed her tune, I think.

We keep the poop wrapped in an old towel, shoved deep in the closet, way back on the top shelf, among my sweaters, like a gun, or jewelry.

Sometimes Heidi comes searching with me. We camouflage our faces with green and black paint. We wear military fatigues and strap high-power rifles to our backs like second spines. Fifty paces apart, we stalk the Yale Reservoir in Southern Washington, the Mt. Hood Wilderness just outside Portland, at sunrise and at twilight—his most active hours—paying close attention to the moon phases and weather patterns.

There is a science to it.

I make Heidi wear a whistle in case she sees anything, in case she's in trouble. She calls me crazy. Says I need to chill out. But all the same, I know she is thankful for the whistle. Sometimes she blows it by accident, when a coyote leaps over a log or when a deer, with a white flash of tail, slips between the trees. And sometimes she blows it just to test me, to see how fast I can run.

Theory: I believe he is a leftover caveman.

I am a big fish in a small pond of people. If something happens, I get the call. I get news of about a dozen sightings a month, all up and down the Cascade Mountains, which split Oregon like a fence. His latest haunt is the Deschutes National Forest, near Sisters, where huckleberry patches go bare, where chicken and sheep go missing, where folks report opening their fridge and finding it not as well stocked as they remembered, sans Budweiser, sans milk and butter, and missing from their spice rack: paprika and cumin, garlic salt, black pepper.

He has been busy.

The other night an enormous creature—enormous like you wouldn't believe—shambled across the interstate, caught before the headlights of a bus full of screaming band kids, their headlights making him golden-eyed, wild, mythic, a monster, and before he shambled into the forest, back to his secret camp, he raised a broad black hand to shield his face.

Your standard fuzzy photograph.

There is a CD called *The Sounds of Sasquatch*. It contains a recording of what is supposedly a Bigfoot call, along with the spelling and pronunciation and suspected meaning of over 400 Bigfoot vocalizations.

"Yum-à-kwa" is how he says hello.

"Yum-a-kwa," Heidi says.

"More oomph to the A," I say and pretend not to notice her rolling her eyes.

"Yum-à-kwa," she says.

"Better," I say.

You should hear this CD, the Bigfoot call in particular. It is powerful, unafraid, unfurling like some black and terrible worm, every note so saturated with bass it would take two large men to pick up and carry. Pretty much how you would expect a leftover caveman to sound: spooky.

We play the CD at full blast, with the windows down, when rocketing along logging roads all over the Pacific Northwest. I know he can hear us, and that it is only a matter of time.

Sometimes it feels as if someone is watching, listening, and I wonder, beyond the window, in the pine forest surrounding my home, where the shadows fuse together, is it him? Is he studying me? Committing to memory, like some shaggy anthropologist, my eating and sexual habits, my favorite television programs, so that when we finally meet, he will know what he is up against?

In the dead of night, when the motion detector clicks on and fills the yard with a yellowish glow, I put on my slippers and I walk outside, onto the deck, toting my thirty-aught-six, and say in an almost whisper, "Yum-à-kwa, Yum-à-kwa, Yum-à-kwa," again and again, like a conjurer's spell.

The call comes at 8:30 pm.

"It's him," the voice says. "He's here."

This is Russ. Russ is vice-president of the Oregon chapter of the Pacific Northwest Bigfooting Society. He lives about thirty miles away, in Rhododendron, and last week rented a backhoe to dig a pit—nearly twenty feet deep, if you can believe it—in the middle of his front yard. He lowered into it buckets of fresh blackberries and raw hamburger, to lure Bigfoot, alongside a couple cowbells, to announce his capture. Then, like something out of a Tarzan episode, he covered the thing with sticks and grass.

"It worked?" I say. "The pit?" I admit I had my doubts. If Bigfoot is anything, he is a climber.

"Bingo!" he says, as if he just netted the Virgin Mary. "Jackpot!"

"You're sure?"

"There's something in there. Something big."

I let loose an Indian war-whoop. It is all I can do to contain my excitement. When I hang up the phone and snatch my keys and head for the door, Heidi asks where on earth am I going and why on earth am I grinning like an idiot.

False alarm, it turns out. I stand at the lip of the pit and with a magnum flashlight spotlight its bottom, revealing a black bear—its eyes glowing green—as it slurps and smacks at its burger-and-berry casserole dinner. The smell—of wet fur and rotten meat—is so ugly it's awe-inspiring. Russ stands behind me, his face pinched with emotion, regarding the bear like a mourner at a funeral.

"For crying out loud," I say. "You make me drive all the way out here for this?"

"Sorry," he says. "I heard the cowbells and I heard this weird groaning and I figured *who else* could it be?" He holds out his hands as if he has given up searching f or something. "I'm stupid. I'm sorry."

When I return home, when I shuffle up the stairs, my shoulders heavy and weighing me down in a disa-ppointed slouch, I find Heidi fast asleep, looking like an Indian burial mound, a body enveloped by a brown blanket. The only sound is the slow whistle of her brea-thing.

I brush my teeth and notice the bath mat, the towel, are damp, the shower dappled with water. Heidi never takes a shower at night. She hates going to bed with wet hair.

Weird.

The moon is out and puddles of it are in the bed-room. A cold puff of breeze slides in the open window and my hair goes prickly. Something is funny. As in not right. I know this sounds corny, but swear to God, I think I've got a sixth sense about me. Just yesterday I was thinking about Chinese food when *bam*: Heidi walks in the door with Egg Foo Yuck.

Now this. Now my body vibrates like a tuning fork when I move to the window and discover in its pane a knot of hair. Rough reddish hair. I bring it to my mouth, slowly, to taste. It tastes like Bigfoot. You might wonder, how does Bigfoot taste? I'll tell you: heavy, mushroomy, like something rotten found in a dank cave. *Evil.*

There is no question about it: *he* has been here. In this bedroom. With my wife.

My heart does a little jumpstart and I consider grabbing her, shaking her, saying, “Wake up!” With a far-off look in her eyes, she would rise from her sleep and say, “What? What’s wrong?” looking around, her mind muddled by dreams.

Outside the motion detector clicks on and reveals something in my brain, bright with the yellow of clarity, a memory from last week, when I snuck up on Heidi taking a shower and peeled back the curtain and discovered her kissing her own hand—passionately, not like the pecks we normally exchange—her eyes closed, her feet twirling her in slow circles as if dancing.

I did not interrupt her then just as I do not wake her now, despite all the questions looping through my mind. In the morning we will talk. For now the truth can wait.

I slump against the wall and feel something empty opening inside me, a hollowness that keeps expanding, leaving behind a cavity’s ache. Partnering this is the overwhelming desire to rip off my clothes and run outside, my wild black shape moving across the lawn and into the woods, howling.

Winter's Trappings

There was a stretch of highway, just outside Sisters, Oregon, where semis—with their engines roaring, their grills gleaming silver—came rumbling down from the Cascade Mountains, a long steep descent, and slammed into deer, dragging them sometimes thirty feet, tearing them open. This happened all the time—three, five times a day—so often that great blood puddles dappled the asphalt, and the buzzards, the ravens, and the magpies would roost in the nearby pines, waiting, descending like some horrible shrieking cloud to pick apart a carcass immediately after it was laid down.

It was as if some *thing* within the deer—some internal bearing, some urge—as inborn as a pulse, drove them from the forest, here.

Here, around midnight one November, Gordon and his mother Pamela hit the buck. They were racing away from Salem, toward Redmond, in their Dodge pickup—its color, once red, now a collage of rust and gray primer—when out of the darkness sprang three deer, two of them does, the last a four-horn buck, caught mid-leap, surrounded by the anemic yellow of halogen headlights.

The buck was a big broad-chested animal, and when the pickup struck him, the impact snapped Gordon forward, snapping his nose against the glove compartment, breaking it. The pop of cartilage separating from bone was lost against the enormous thud of metal and meat.

Pamela mashed the brake and the tires squealed and the pickup lurched and the buck rolled over the hood—slick with snow from the mountain pass—over the windshield, the cab, its antlers and hooves clattering, its body finally thumping into the bed just as the pickup came to a rocking halt.

"Jesus," Pamela said, "Christ."

Gordon made a little yelp and tented his hands over his nose, to stop the blood, to muffle the pain, which was like nothing he had ever known in his twelve years. He had broken fingers, fallen from trees and dirt bikes, torn off his toenail, lost a tooth in a fistfight, felt innumerable times his father's hand's sting, but this…this was something new. It was as if here, now, for the first time, he had finally been introduced to what he had only glimpsed the edges of before: pain, real pain, a roaring burn that fingered its way behind his eyes and up his forehead, pinching his brain with sharp fingernails.

Later on, when he had time to think about it, Gordon realized that if you took the way he felt when his father, during one of his drunks, tripped his mother down the stairs, when he took off his belt and whipped her face with the buckle, if you took that vision and melted it into a physical sensation, a broken nose would be it.

Now Gordon was crying, but not like he normally cried, with big gulping hiccups. He knew that would only make the pain worse. Silently, awfully, he let the tears drop down his cheeks, cleaning paths through the blood. When his mother asked, "You okay, baby?" he took a hand from his nose, showed her the blood, and quickly returned it. "I'm sorry," she said, "Jesus, I'm so sorry," though her voice was distant and seemed not to refer to his injury, but to something else entirely.

She sighed through her nose, took her foot off the brake, and the pickup crawled forward, maybe a little wheezy, with one headlight busted, but otherwise no worse for wear. She parked on the cinder shoulder and twisted the ignition quiet and they sat there a moment, breathing. A Wal-Mart semi rushed past, moaning as it downshifted, swaying their pickup with the woosh of air it had displaced.

They left the doors open, the keys buzzing in the ignition, and stepped around front to investigate the damage and stepped around back to investigate the cause. "We are so lucky," Pamela said in a tone that reminded Gordon of the church people on TV: desperate to convince. "This could have been much, much worse."

All this time Gordon kept his hands pressed to his nose, as if to stifle a sneeze, breathing through his mouth. The alpine air tasted clean and cold and brought gray clouds from his lungs, smearing the stars and the planets that wheeled above, so ancient and deep with energy, so vast. He had forgotten about stars, living in Salem, where the neon signs and street lamps drowned away their light. Just then a constellation broke apart, a star descended, flaring greenly into nothingness. He imagined he heard its sizzle.

His mother was nibbling at her thumbnail, as was her habit, focusing her eyes on the pickup bed. Gordon climbed onto the bumper for a better view and saw some Styrofoam coffee cups and two plastic suitcases they had hurriedly filled earlier that evening after his father pressed a too-rare T-bone steak to his mother's mouth, holding it there, strangling her with it until Gordon stabbed him in the arm with a fork and said, "Stop!"

And on top of the suitcases, all splayed out, was the buck, its neck at a funny angle. Gordon could feel the heat coming off it, but couldn't smell it, could smell and taste only the color red, such a lovely and terrifying color. The dome-light reflected off the buck's eye, brightening it into an orange sun, making Gordon wonder, just for a moment, was it alive, was it watching him? Then he saw how its tongue hung from its mouth—so purple—like a coughed-up ventricle.

His mother touched his shoulder, squeezed it, turning him, shepherding him back into the pickup. "Come on," she said, "We're almost there," her voice a ragged and somehow cheerful thing. "Nothing we can do now except leave it be. Verna will be happy for the meat."

She was referring to her sister, who lived on thirty acres of sage and conifers near the lower Metolius River. Fifteen minutes later they knocked on her cabin door, its brass knob worn bright as gold, and when it opened, some buttery light filtered around her edges but basically she filled the entire doorway.

The next morning Gordon woke with his cousins, Rita and Rachel, standing over him. They were sixteen and they were twins. They were not particularly attractive, nor were they ugly. Plain and rigid, like Amish furniture, they wore pageboy haircuts and their expressions never changed, not really, from the clinical stare they gave Gordon now, the same stare they gave him a few years back, when they demanded to see his penis.

Gordon had said, "Are you kidding?"

"No," they had said. "Now show us."

He wouldn't, so they made him. This happened deep in the woods, where they had led him, where no one could hear him cry out. They were big girls, not fat, but husky—like Aunt Verna—stronger than Gordon, who adults often called a beanpole. Rita held him down on a blond bed of pine needles while Rachel yanked his shorts around his ankles.

"It's so small," Rita said.

"It's so pink," Rachel said. "I'm reminded of a boiled shrimp."

"Weird," they said.

Now he lay balled up on the couch, cocooned beneath an afghan, the dull ache of his nose reminding him of last night. He could hear bacon hissing in a pan, the coffeemaker burbling and popping, but he could smell nothing. His nose was clogged with gelatinous blood. The twins snapped their eyes at him, studying him, their arms crossed beneath their muscular breasts. One of them—Rachel, he thought—finally said, "Greetings, cousin."

Rita said, "Mother tells us you'll be staying for awhile."

Rachel said, "Have you looked at yourself in the mirror? You look like crap."

And he did. The bathroom mirror revealed an eggplant purple reached up the swollen length of his nose, making a raccoon's mask around his eyes, all bloodshot and sore, his lashes rooted in yellow sleep scabs.

Aunt Verna was the very definition of butch. She wore steel-toed boots and denim—always denim—denim pants, denim shirts, denim jackets with wool collars, denim of all different colors, maybe even denim underpants, for all Gordon knew. She didn't wear makeup, didn't dye her hair, but wore it in a grayish sort of crew cut, only long in back. His father called her The Mullet. He called her other things, too, but never to her face. He didn't dare. She was twice the size of him, just about, her muscles like small sacks of grain, full and surging beneath her clothes. When she was younger, she had traveled around, competing in arm-wrestling tournaments, and to this day kept the medals and trophies hanging in her study, among her diplomas, so many you could have hammered them into a suit of golden armor.

Once, when she was trying to loosen a rusted-over lug nut, Gordon saw her break a wrench. And another time, when she brought him along to see about a sick bull—she was a vet—he watched in amazement when she slugged the animal for trying to hoove her, slugged it right in the snout, sending the bull into a sneezing fit.

She had always seemed an invincible kind of woman, the kind who filled up a room, who never looked small, not even from a distance, not even when dwarfed by the Cascades. Like the sky, she was enormous, everyone craning their necks to pay her attention. And so whenever Gordon visited his her cabin, he felt safe. He felt good.

He wasn't sure he believed it, but his mother claimed a man hurt Verna long ago. Not physically—she never would have allowed that—but the man tore her heart open, gashed it, leaving it scarred over with gummy white tissue, impenetrable. When Gordon heard this, he tried to imagine his aunt with a man, and couldn't. The vision seemed wrong to him, incongruous, as mismatched as a butcher knife in a Christmas stocking. What seemed more believable was that by some miraculous process the twins had appeared one morning, crawling out of a hole in the earth, brushing the dirt off their sleeves, waving hello.

But Verna had been hurt, just as his mother had been hurt. You could see it in both their faces, the straightness of their spines, though they handled their hurt differently. His mother would stand where she hoped no one would see her, wearing an absent headachy expression, her head bowed, seemingly bent by the weight of the gray winter sky; whereas Verna would take the center of the room, the head of the table, her feet planted wide, her hands gesturing in quick tomahawk motions, her eyes sparkling with something like joy and malice, as she was now, at breakfast, when shoveling a forkful of egg into her mouth. "If that son of a bitch was here, you know what I'd do? I'd cut his neck. And then I'd cut him up into little pink cubes. I'd heat up a pot and boil him in it for a whole day. I'd season him with some wild peppermint and some onion and basil. Maybe I'd put some dried berries in with him, some roots and some potatoes, make him into a stew." All this time she kept her eyes sharp on Gordon, as if daring him to grow into such a man as his father.

Pamela shook her head and put a trembly hand to her forehead, rubbing the space between her eyebrows.

"Jesus, Verna."

Verna assumed a mock-innocent expression. "What?"

"You really think Gordon needs to hear that kind of thing?"

She made a dismissive gesture with her hand. "Bah," she said. "He knows his old man is a worthless pile of shit, don't you, Gordon?" When Gordon said nothing, she popped her eyebrows and said, "Don't you?"

Now Gordon hurried to agree with her, saying, "Yes, ma'am," though he wasn't sure how he felt about his father. Sometimes he wanted to kill him, and sometimes he wanted to hug him. It was complicated. The man had a switch inside him—of that Gordon was certain—a switch whose triggering caught him in a kind of private darkness, from which he would emerge the next morning—his eyes red-rimmed with regret—apologizing to them believably, profusely, with roses the color of skinned knees, bottles of peppery red wine, kisses.

In a way, Gordon felt sorry for him, imagining him last night, after he came home from Slippery's Tavern, smelling of cigarettes and beer, of peanuts scooped from peanut boats, walking through every room, twice, three times, calling their names louder and louder and receiving no reply, because they were gone, they were some two hundred miles away and at that very moment showing Verna the buck, broken and motionless in the back of the pickup.

"Well, isn't that the damndest thing," she had said. One of its hind legs stuck out at a sharp angle and she took it by the hoof, lifted it, let it fall. "Quite polite of him, wasn't it? He knew exactly where to go. Like a dollar into the offering plate." She dropped the tailgate and crawled up into the bed, yanking the stag by the antlers, wrestling his limp body off their luggage, now spotted with blood.

"No sense messing around this time of night," she said. "I'll be up again in a couple hours. The cold will keep him until then."

After breakfast, when Gordon's mother called the Dodge dealership where she worked as a secretary, where her husband worked as a salesman, and told them she wouldn't be coming in, not today, not for a while—maybe not ever—the twins washed dishes and Aunt Verna wrestled her way into a pair of Carhartt coveralls, not much too big for her body, her body as solid and ruddy as roast beef. "Come on then," she said and ruffled Gordon's hair. "I'll show you a thing or two about being a man."

He followed her to the garage, where she sharpened a knife, sliding its long blue blade along a piece of novaculite, a finely granular, highly pure silica rock mined only in Arkansas, she claimed. "Doesn't chew away the metal like all those diamond-hone electric gadgets." She was always saying things like this, handing out nuggets of wisdom like strange candy.

She sharpened the knife slowly, diagonally, making a low scraping sound, and when its edge was "sharp enough to split an atom," she set it down on a stainless steel counter with an industrial sink. "We'll slice him open," she said with energy, her tongue wetting her lips, "and then we'll hang him high." From a pulley system above a central floor drain, she lowered a hook the size of a hand. "You are not going to believe the amount of goop a deer has inside it. It's kind of extraordinary."

She hauled up the garage door and it settled above them with a rusty rattling bang. Sunlight filled the air, highlighting the dust whirling in every direction. They headed outside, walking toward the pickup, their feet making chewed-ice sounds on the gravel. The air seemed flavored with the promise of snow, thin and aspirinic.

It wasn't until Aunt Verna stopped and said, "Well, hell," balling her hands against her bulky hips, that Gordon noticed the buck. It stood in the pickup's bed—one of its legs curled up under it, like a flamingo—looking right at them so that Gordon froze, afraid and awed, admiring its reddish tan coat, its wide rack, with eight white points rising out of a brown crown. It swished its black tail and a cool breeze blew and they stood this way a long time, looking at each other.

Then the buck approached the open tailgate and more fell, than jumped off it, landing clumsily, sort of collapsing and bawling over some secret pain inside, before righting itself and taking off at a crooked run that lasted about twenty feet, and then its legs crumpled, its chin hit the ground, and it rolled on its side and quit.

Clouds piled up on the mountains and the world turned cold. Sap slowed in the pine trees, seizing up for winter, crystallizing like the blood of dormant frogs, and the last leaves fell from the sumac and alder and cottonwood to scatter around the cabin—the leaves looking like gold coins, like something whose core contained riches, maybe chocolate—and Aunt Verna told Gordon and the twins to rake them into piles for burning. Flames rose, crackling into giant orange tongues that licked Gordon's skin so hot he took one step back, then another.

Rain fell and froze and surrounded the crabgrass and the yellow fennel with a thin white film that crunched beneath Gordon's boots, when he walked around these thirty acres, exploring, seeing. Seeing a bobcat slink off between the trees, a coyote leap over a log, a great horned owl swoop from its perch, its wings silent as it snatched a chipmunk and sailed off to some secret destination to eviscerate the dinner caught between its claws. Seeing his mother chewing her thumb, stripping the flesh off it, until it bled, seeing her doll up her face with excess trashy makeup, seeing her head off to interviews—"Cross your fingers," she said, "and hold your breath."—seeing her tremendous face-splitting grin when she came home with a secretary position at the chamber of commerce. Seeing Aunt Verna nurse the broken buck back to health, corralling him out back, splinting his fore and hind legs, draining with a syringe his joints, all swollen with puss, feeding him alfalfa, apples, corn, IGH pellets made of oats, hormones, and bone-meal.

She was like a painter, in that she spoke of the buck as if he were a rough sketch on a canvas—"Such beautiful lines," she would say, watching him limp around the split-rail enclosure—tending to his improvement in small careful doses, not wanting to rush his release into the world. She was never so gentle as she was with him, going *sh-sh-sh* to calm him when she brushed back his fur, revealing the darker silkier coat beneath. She named him Lazarus and eventually he came to recognize his name.

The twins beat the hoarfrost off the logs with a broom and with an ax split wood for hours, never tiring, pausing only to position a log so that the blade might follow the grain, sliding, severing, with no more effort than they beat up the boys who beat up Gordon when he enrolled at the local junior-and-senior high school. The ones in letterman jackets and expensive white sneakers surrounded and ravaged him—a fawn among wolves—but the twins always came to his rescue, their faces calm but flushed with blood when they performed a right cross, an uppercut, a one-two combination followed by a roundhouse swing—as their mother taught them, punching *through* their target, with one foot planted before the other for stability—their movement and noise as violent as the sharp crack of the broken wood they gathered and stacked in a rectangular pile so tall they needed a stepladder to reach its top.

Shadows turned bluer, spreading, joining together like rising water. Ice worked its way along the edges of a nearby pond where rainbow trout slept in beds of frozen mud and after school sometimes the twins would take him here. They would wear mackinaws and gumboots and stocking caps and they would set up lawn chairs on the shore and sip hot cider from steel thermoses and toss rocks through the ice, watching for how long it took to heal over.

Late at night the phone would ring. Sometimes it was a rancher—calling about a fevered colt, a fresh heifer bleeding from her udders—and sometimes it was not. Sometimes it was Gordon's father, his voice so violent it carried across two hundred miles of cable, dripping from the pores of the receiver to the floor, where it slid across the kitchen linoleum, the living room hardwood, finding Gordon on the couch, his makeshift bedroom until he and his mother could afford their own place, something better.

Gordon pictured his father sitting on their kitchen counter back in Salem, surrounded by dirty dishes, crumpled beer cans, empty bags of off-brand potato chips—fruit flies swirling everywhere—his mouth pursed as he waited for the rhythmic purr of the call to be broken by a "Hello?" He would not say, "What's up?" or "I'm sorry." He would scream. A forked vein would leap across his forehead and he would beg them to come back, promising to love them if they did, threatening to kill them if they didn't. Did Pamela not realize she had embarrassed him at work, where all day people pointed and spoke her name from behind cupped hands? Did she not realize she had effectively kidnapped his son? *His* son.

He never noticed that the line had gone dead, that Verna had gently taken the phone from Pamela and set it in its cradle and unplugged it, so focused was he on his own noise—his throat pumping out the poison inside him until it was all gone.

The pickup knocked something from Lazarus—some of his wildness—leaving it behind for the magpies to eat, like a limb in a trap. He became dependent, and when the water froze or when the corral went empty of alfalfa, he would bawl the shrill rasping cry of steam released quickly from the earth, of dinosaurs, things long buried. "Take care of it," Verna would say to Gordon and watch him through the kitchen window when he went into the cold to stomp open the veneer of ice collecting on the water trough.

At first Lazarus feared him, hobbling off to the far edge of the corral with his ears flattened against his skull, swirling his antlers in a clockwise motion to show he was ready for Gordon. Once Lazarus even snapped his mouth, as if to bite, when he charged Gordon and turned away at the last minute to circle back to his original position. But eventually—as eventually as you might grow accustomed to a neighbor with a hideous deformity—Lazarus grew accustomed to Gordon and to Verna and would lower his crown as if in thanks when they fed him, petted him, finding with their fingers that special place between his ears he loved so much.

By now Gordon's nose had healed and he could smell, and he would smell his hand long after he pet Lazarus, like a teenage lover, enjoying the wet-dog old-leather odor left behind.

Trapping would put Rita and Rachel through college. They trapped beavers and otters and pine marten, had done so for the past ten years in the Conibear 330 traps they set along the Squaw River, which poured and purled through their property, frozen in places, entombing the traps in blue ice.

In the garage they would skin and flesh the animals, their blood hosed in pink frothing waves down the central floor drain, which would emit a final gurgling burp as if in satisfaction. The furs were then flattened and nailed to a board with one hundred nails. These hung throughout the garage, circular and wafer-thin and looking as though they had been steamrolled or dropped from a great height.

"Prices aren't as good as they were in the 80's," the twins would say, "but we aren't complaining." Otters were worth around ninety dollars, beavers less, much less, averaging eighteen dollars, with the occasional monster pelt pulling in twenty-five from the fur-buying cooperatives in Canada, which took a nine-percent commission. Right now the twins were stocking up for January, for the North American Fur Auction, where most of their sales would go to Chinese or Russian furriers.

This two-degree day in December they took Gordon with them, through the frozen fields and forest, where dim light fell through the ribs of trees and the dry powdery snow squeaked beneath their boots, packed into something slick and blue. Rita carried a backpack filled with tools and ham sandwiches and peppered jerky and a thermos of hot cocoa and Rachel dragged behind her an orange plastic sled that smoothed her tracks, only to be broken a moment later by Gordon and then Lazarus, Lazarus trailing by twenty yards and pausing whenever they paused, maintaining the distance between them.

The other day they had tried to set him free. They had opened the corral and he had lifted his head from his drinking trough. Water dribbled from his muzzle when he regarded the gate and beyond it, the forest. But he did not prance off into the distance, as they expected, wild and free, not even when they crept back to cabin to watch with their faces pressed to the windows, every minute or so wiping away the frost their breath created. Instead Lazarus returned to his drinking and then bedded down on a blanket of straw, plumper and happier than he had ever been.

"That deer," Verna had said, "is a chicken."

In the days after, with the gate still yawning open, Lazarus would venture into the surrounding meadow, pawing through the snow for grass, occasionally staring off at the surrounding pines, their needles coated with white frosting, and he would cock his head, as if listening. Aunt Verna once told Gordon a dog's nose is 220 million times more sensitive than a human's. He wondered if it worked the same with ears—the stag's ears as big as a big beach shell—and what Lazarus could hear with them—the shushing boom of an avalanche, a black bear murmuring in its winter sleep, gunshots shouting from the faraway hills, or more than that? The throb and hiss of a hibernating grub's black guts? The sap crawling along a juniper's roots? The rush of a trout parting the water beneath the ice? Or maybe something darker, more sinister, some undersound, a whisper that reminded him of the cannibalism of the wilderness, and how he ought to stay put, stay here, under Aunt Verna's meaty wing, where life seemed a safe and good thing.

Now Lazarus kept his crown low, trying to melt into the underbrush, watching the woods with the same wariness as before—as if seeking that part of himself which had been left behind—never straying from the sled-polished tracks of Gordon and the twins.

From time to time, Gordon noticed, a jackrabbit or a magpie or a coyote would stick their head from beneath a thicket, from behind a pine, and stare—just for a moment—at the bizarre parade of man and beast, before hurrying off.

Gordon heard the Squaw's whisper before he saw it, appearing suddenly before them, a broad blue snake dusted with snow, the water as hushed beneath its ice-skin as blood. Tendrils of fog swirled up and down its length, as if rising from secret chimneys, their steam slowly burning away under the sun's white glare.

"Here we are," Rita said and stepped onto the river, carefully, sliding more than stepping toward where the tips of aspen branches jutted through the ice and marked the beaver colony's feed bed. Farther down the river, in a hump of sticks that might have been some enormous creature laid down to rest, was the lodge.

Rita shrugged off her backpack and removed from it a chisel. "Your turn to chip," she said, and Rachel said, "I know," snatching the chisel, irritated maybe, though it was hard to tell since she spoke in such Vulcan tones. "Don't tell me what I already know."

Rita said, deadpan, "It's sunny. It's cold. It's December."

"I am not amused," Rachel said and dropped to her knees, chipping with short powerful chops through three inches of ice, the shaving sticking to her mittens, while Gordon ate a snowball as if it were an apple, nibbling it down to a pulpy core. The sound of the chisel went ticking and snapping around the empty room of the morning. At one point Rachel paused to remove her stocking cap and shove it in her coat pocket, her hair damp with sweat and steaming in the cold, soon hardening into an icy helmet, as she attacked the river once more and in a violent succession of stabs finally broke through and the water boiled up like a grayish tea that splashed and froze on her gloves.

Once the twins widened the hole wide enough to accommodate the trap, they pulled it from the dark water. Inside the steel square was a beaver, dead, its mahogany fur slick and gleaming, its tail ridiculous, its mouth open, displaying long orange scimitars for teeth. "This one's a good one," Rachel said, "a twenty-pounder," when she rolled it in the snow to absorb the water from its coat. She then dumped it in the sled with its little legs stuck up in the air, frozen in a pose of defense, as if ready to catch something thrown at it.

Gordon looked at Lazarus—who was looking at the beaver—and wondered what the stag was thinking. Thinking about the steel jaws of the Dodge pickup bearing down on him. Thinking about the cage of his corral. *Thinking*. Maybe Gordon gave the animal too much credit. There was just so much personality in its eyes, so gloomy and black and regarding him with thankfulness or fear, he didn't know.

Rachel pointed her mitten at Rita and said, "Pull."

"I always pull the sled. Why don't you pull the sled?"

"Why don't you kiss my butt?"

"I know," Rita said. "Gordon will pull it." They stared

at him, snapping their eyelids, their faces revealing nothing.

"No way," he said. "You're the ones making money off it."

The twins' voices were sober and motherly when they said, "We provide you with food and shelter, Gordon. It's the least you could do."

A great honking introduced a flock of geese before they appeared, flying low, just over the trees, so low Gordon could see their black eyes reflecting all the whiteness spread beneath them. When they disappeared, headed south, somewhere warmer and greener and better than wherever they escaped, he looked at the twins, looked away, looked again at their broad expectant faces and said, "Fine," and took the towline and dragged the sled up the trail, his footsteps sliding away from him in the snow, as if he was incapable of moving forward without being drawn back, reminded of the way he came.

The day Gordon's father arrived was the day a freezing rain fell, following three days of snow, the rain glazing a blue-white sheet across Central Oregon like the frosting on an expensive cake whose powdery core measured two feet deep. Branches shattered. Light glowed from every corner of the world. Cars slipped and flipped, into ditches, into other cars, while the semis plodded along slowly, powerfully, like brontosauruses bent on their migration, one of them crumpling a spun-out Geo beneath its chain-choked wheels, the news reporter said while the tickertape at the bottom of the screen announced school cancellations throughout

Deschutes County.

That morning the twins set off on their Polaris snowmobile, breaking through the ice and then cresting it and then breaking through again in the slow violent rhythm of a ship in rough water, headed to Sisters to shovel the driveways of anyone willing to cough up twenty dollars.

That morning Gordon discovered it was possible, if he tiptoed, to walk across the two-inch crust without breaking through. With each step the ice squeaked and groaned, settling under his weight—and he imagined there was nothing to catch him if he punched through, nothing except snow for miles and miles beneath him, and so at any moment he might plummet into a forever whiteness where snow sharks and snow snakes slid around, hunting.

Behind him Verna chipped and dug a trail from the garage to the corral, where Lazarus—whose tiny hooves punctured the ice—crashed through with every panicked step he took, so that his legs bled, bright red, and he bawled for help, for Verna to once again clean his wounds and butter them with salve.

If Gordon and Verna had not been so focused on their task—whispering to the stag, petting him as they led him into the garage, limping and mewling, the muscles jumping beneath his fur—if they had *only* looked a quarter mile to the west, lifting their hands to their hairlines as visors, they would have seen the black Dodge Ram slowly turn into the driveway and slowly carve a path toward the cabin, like some Antarctic vessel, exposing in its wake a track of blue peppered with red cinders unstuck from its tires' tread.

As it was, Gordon and Verna did not look—closing the door behind them with a *click*—nor did they hear the diesel engine go quiet, the footsteps on the porch, the soft knock at the door and the undoing of the bolt to answer it. The garage radio was tuned to KICE 100 and Gordon snapped his fingers and Verna sang, in her gruff barking way, along with Woody Guthrie as he described the five shades of shadow that darken the land.

No, they didn't realize they had a visitor at all until thirty minutes later, when they entered the cabin through the garage, walked down the hall and noticed a sound, as bright as sun-struck snow, seeping from the guest room—Pamela's room.

That sounds like quail, Gordon thought, quail calling to each other. The lilting croon accompanied the creak and zoop of springs, the clacking of the headboard against the wall—and it only took him a second to understand. Verna saw the understanding swell into a smile that bent into a frown that settled into the restrained suspicious expression he learned from the twins.

"Come on, son," she said and laid on his shoulder her heavy mitt of a hand. "Let's you and me go cook some lunch, huh?"

Gordon's father—who people called Buddy—had driven all night, driving straight from the dealership off Kuebler toward the mountains, up and down the Santiam Pass, stopping only for gas. His blood fizzed with caffeine—not booze, not ever again, he had decided, taking pull after frantic pull from a one-liter bottle of

Coca-Cola clamped between his thighs. He had no plan. He only knew he had to get there, get them.

Once he hit the pass, where the sleet wrapped ice mittens around his wipers and where the taillights of other cars, lost cars, glowed redly from the ditches, he couldn't go more than twenty-miles-an-hour. At one point, way up high, in the snowy saddle between Three-Fingered Jack and Hoodoo, a perilous place where the winds came pouring along at a howl, his brakes locked and he slipped off the road, only to be towed out two hours later by a cinder truck. And at another point he ran over a fawn—watched it slip, heard the thump, felt the truck rise on its left side—but could do nothing as it happened on an incline so slick and so steep that if he were to stop, he might never move forward again.

And finally—*finally*—after twenty-four hours awake and painfully sober, he showed up on the front porch, his lungs pumping—like a stag in rut—his eyes wide and rolling around in their sockets, when he handed Pamela flowers, roses whose petals had wilted and blackened from ten hours before his blazing heat vents.

More than a month had passed since they last saw each other, and he immediately noticed in Pamela something different, something Verna. Whereas before she had always appeared a little cadaverous, as gray and sickly as wet concrete, she had put on color and weight. She looked less slump-shouldered, more big-butted. Even her wrists seemed different, more rounded, her veins expanding to drink the golden harvest of this place, this healing place, so far from any city.

After she took the flowers from him and threw them

over his shoulder, into the day, she turned on her heel, but left the door open, a sort of invitation. In the living room she crossed her arms and uncrossed them and looked everywhere but his face—too square-jawed and too green-eyed to reason with—when he said his *I'm sorry's* and *Never again's* and *Would you please please* please *forgive me's* and touched her face with the back of his hand, his lumpy knuckles familiar there and as effective as any punch in giving him power, making her his. It was that easy. She was like an animal wanting to be coaxed into light. And when they went to the bedroom, kissing hard and knocking against the walls, she felt pleasured by the rough play, all her good sense and all Verna's good advice obscured when they laid down.

Pamela emerged from the bedroom, a drugged smile on her face, to find Verna and Gordon busy in the kitchen, warming a pot of corn chowder and slicing honey-cured ham for sandwiches. The look shared between the sisters was one of private understanding and old grudges.

"You're so dumb," Verna said, breathing fiercely through her nostrils, and Pamela said, "I know," but didn't stop smiling.

"What do you want on your sandwich," Verna said and pointed the knife at her. "Tomato? Onion?" The knife caught the light streaming in the window and bounced it across the ceiling. Gordon watched it there before turning his attention back to his mother.

"Yes. That sounds good." Pamela leaned her elbows on the slate counter dividing the dining nook and kitchen, making eyes with Gordon. “Your daddy’s here.”

When Gordon didn’t answer—not knowing what to say —Verna stabbed her knife into the mustard jar, a little rough in her slopping yellow across a slice of wheat bread, and said, “He’s not stupid. Not like you.”

“Gordon?” Pamela said. “Would you like to see him?”

Verna said, “Whose house is this? This is my house.”

Pamela’s voice was a high-pitched and desperate thing when she said, “He’s better, I swear. He swears, too.” This was the first time Gordon considered his mother pathetic. “He swears he’s done drinking, Verna.”

Verna considered her a moment, snorted like a mare after a hot run, and returned to her sandwiches.

Just then a door clicked open and footsteps came down the hall and Buddy emerged from it, smiling, wearing his best salesman outfit—a JC Penney suit, black with gray pinstripes and gold cufflinks and a too-big gold watch shimmering around his wrist—looking rumpled but slick. “Hey, Gordo,” he said. “Good to see you, buddy. You got a hug for me?”

For a second Gordon forgot who his father was and remembered who he had been, remembering all the times they lounged on the couch, half-asleep, watching football and eating peanuts and cussing imaginatively when the Ducks lost to a field goal in O.T. In those days Gordon never believed there would come a time when his father wouldn’t be laughing, telling stories about the people he knew, the things he did, the milk-white Camero he drove in high school, even when two beers turned into six beers turned into twelve beers, even when the alcohol seemed to pull his gaze further and further away, even when darkness grew against the windows and meanness slipped from his mouth as easy as rain off a leaf, even when he hurled a nacho platter against the wall and left behind a bouquet of guacamole and salsa.

Even then.

Back then Gordon understood on some level something was going to happen, something was going to end, but didn't *believe*.

Once, nearly a year ago, after everyone else had gone to bed, Gordon drank from a bottle of Southern Comfort. Its taste, like the smell of fireworks, was recognizable but unlike anything he had ever put in his body. It had a different heat to it, so that his skin opened every pore a bit wider to sigh away its steam, or else risk burning. Not five swigs and he felt all of a sudden soft—as if his bones had fallen out—and he felt the need to vomit, and did, and felt happy for it because what happened to his father—the rage, the insatiable thirst—had not happened to him.

Now his father looked like he used to look, on his good days, smiling a wide teeth-showing smile, his arms open, requesting a hug; but Gordon's many memories did battle like wind currents and ultimately the frozen air overwhelmed any lingering warmth, as he remembered his mother spitting bits of tooth, the black marks smudged across his back, the way his father sometimes seemed wrapped up in a fiery cloud all his own.

And so when his father approached him, Gordon took several steps back until the wall prevented any further escape.

Of course Buddy couldn't *not* drink. It was necessary. It was fundamental. Like breathing. He woke later that night with an awful thirst, with moonlight coming through the window, onto the wall, where it made a silver rectangle. He raised his hand to put a shadow in it. Then he snuck from his bed to his truck and removed from the glove-box a bottle of Wild Turkey and took it to the bathroom to drink, in front of the mirror, as he sometimes did, watching his throat pitch and heave when the burning worked its way inside him, settling in his belly and sending tiny white wasps all up and down his veins.

Outside the world was silent as sleep. On top the forest balanced a full moon, haloing the trees a brilliant blue, its calmness counterpoint to Buddy, who became lycanthropic when he drank, his logic and his kindness dragged from his body and held hostage until dawn. Thirty minutes and he finished half the bottle and flushed the toilet and opened the door and discovered Verna there, a big stooped thing holding his jacket in one hand, a pump-action shotgun in the other. "Get out," she said and tossed him his jacket.

When he started to say something, to explain, to beg her not to tell, to promise this time was the last time, she slowly brought a finger to her lips.

In the moonlight Buddy sang a Merle Haggard song—"I take a lot of pride in what I am."—his voice half wolf, half angel, a baritone drone that lifted Gordon from a dreamless sleep. He rose from the couch and went to the window and saw his father sitting cross-legged in the snow, a bottle rising regularly from his crotch to his mouth, its motion like masturbating.

Gordon flipped a lamp switch and the room filled with a dim yellow color that transformed the window into a sort of mirror that reflected Gordon—shirtless and ribby—and at the same time revealed his father standing and approaching the glass in his crooked way of walking.

They studied each other through the window, the image of Gordon surrounded by the image of his father, a first and last condition, both of them very faintly smiling. Buddy looked at Gordon with troubled eyes, eyes he hoped would tell things he could not otherwise say. There was something in them Gordon did not recognize, some thoughtfulness, some sadness he eventually recognized as goodbye.

Their breathing fogged either side of the glass, obscuring their faces, and they wiped away the fog and continued to stare as sometimes two people will observe each other over a gulf too wide to be bridged, and understand what could have happened, but never will.

That January—after the finalized divorce papers were signed by Buddy, signed by Pamela, and notarized by the Circuit Court of the First Judicial Circuit, Marion County—the twins lit a bonfire.

For the past few weeks Gordon had accompanied them, door-to-door, all over Central Oregon, collecting Christmas trees for five dollars, for their ever-expanding college fund. "Zip up your coat and button your top button," Rita said to Rachel when they rang a doorbell in Redmond. "You look like a tramp."

"Do you want to make money," Rachel said and unzipped her jacket another inch, revealing a canyon of cleavage, "or do you want to make money?"

They made money all right. They made a killing. Even those without trees—the Rosenberg family, the Dewans, the Foos—donated five dollars, twenty, money that gained them admission to the bonfire party, which turned out to be quite the spread, with steaming buckets of cider and hot cocoa, plumped bratwursts and venison sausages stacked on platters, beans, chips, baby carrots, s'mores—and at ten o'clock sharp the twins sparked a match and brought fire to the pyramidal mound of trees, over thirty-feet tall and fifty-feet wide.

The fire started with a sizzle that rose into a popping roar—immediately—the fingers of flame reaching up and up and up, through the branches, scorching the needles into ash the color of snow, until a great orange whip snapped at the night's ceiling and made the air so hot your skin seared, your eyeballs dried out, and the whole world felt made of fire. All snow within a fifty-foot radius vanished and Lazarus darted in and out of the creeping darkness as if simultaneously drawn toward and afraid of the light. Children chased him and laughed and the bones of branches glowed red and cinders tornadoed into the black sky. Little pockets of sap lit up and popped like flashbulbs, crackling out the smell of Christmas, the discarded joy of Christmas trees.

Gordon couldn't help but wonder at the violence of

it all. It was if, each tree were filled with a hidden menace just waiting to get out.

All around him people were cheerful and joking, and he walked among them, brushing against their bodies, listening to their conversations, smiling when he passed his mother, who carried a tray of ciders and who smiled back in a way that revealed she was in pain. He felt sorry for her, always serving others, unequipped for any struggle.

Beyond her, on the other side of the fire, stood her counterpoint, Aunt Verna, who in many ways was beginning to feel like more of a parent than he had ever known. She absentmindedly petted Lazarus while admiring the flames with happiness and confidence and darkness playing across her face the way shadows play across a face staring into a fire.

Gordon discovered it was possible to squint into the flames and at the same time see Verna haloed with light, and in this way she reminded him of the statue—The Golden Pioneer—that graced the capital building in Salem—looking over them all, so impossibly gold.

She saw him watching her and gave him a salute, a snappy gesture with some Marine Core in it, and he waved back—and as the fire grew hotter the night grew brighter and brighter still, as bright as day, and the air burned so you would have thought spring had arrived, and with it, the Chinook winds, which would one day rot the snow blanket covering the ground, making tongue noises as ice quickened into water, forming holes, exposing the brown grass that would grow greener as the holes grew larger until finally all the white would evaporate in gentle heat waves that would reorganize into puffy white clouds that would look, to Gordon, like some part of Heaven.

The Bearded Lady Says Goodnight

The Bearded Lady is dead.

I know this to be true because I pressed my finger to her wrist, and then her neck, and found no pulse. I even touched her eyeball. Nothing. I am the one who called the police, who answered their questions, who showed them the pale body in the tub and listened to them laugh when they hoisted her up, naked and streaming ribbons of water. That was the saddest thing I have ever done. I watched the hole dug in the ground. I watched the pine casket lowered, the first shovel of dirt slap its lid.

She was my sweetheart.

It's complicated. First there's her sensitive disposition. Doesn't matter if her biceps were round as cannonballs. Forget her mean squint, her aggressive smoking of cigarettes. Don't let any of that business fool you.

She wasn't all beard.

Notice instead the pink dress hanging in the closet, the silk panties I take with me to bed, the daisies woven in her hair and the baby powder perfume that lingers long after she's gone. What else? We had good pillow talk, and sometimes she hugged me so tight, so close, her heartbeat seemed to take over mine.

That was The Bearded Lady I loved.

She was my sweetheart, but our love was not without complications. If I am certain of anything in this world, it is this: bearded women are a dangerous and unpredictable lot.

My girl, she had a right hook like a curl of lightning, but it was just as common you'd taste her tears as feel the sharp snap of her knuckles. It all depended. Look at her funny and she might fall to pieces, or else put on a headlock until the capillaries in your eyeballs burst.

Unpredictable.

When the carnival came to Deschutes County, I went for the roller coaster, to eat some fried dough and wieners and cotton candy, to try my hand at the ring toss and maybe win a goldfish or a stuffed bear—but I discovered love instead.

George—a friend, a dude with spectacularly buck teeth—he was there, too. We are a regular pair of nobodys who work as horsemen for the Lazy H outfit. Our stallion, Oregon's Organ, is a golden Buckskin, durably built with gentle temperament and much breeding potential. At this time he had produced only two get, though both were of color. He was, he *is*, the pride of Lazy H and will one day be a legend. Already we have shipped his fluids as far as Texas.

Most of our days are spent grooming, forking straw, breeding quarter horses, herding and branding and castrating cattle, and various other ranchero whathave-yous. The work we do is respectable, pretty much, though sometimes we work with the Mexicans—cleaning stalls, for example. We don't complain. The pay is enough to fill my fridge with Budweiser, to swell my belly with good restaurant food. Most of our nights disappear into playing pool, downing beers at this tavern called Wounded Soldier, where occasionally we ride the mechanical bull.

George's teeth are so bad he can barely manage his lips around them. It is a constant and visible struggle. The way his upper lip quivers, it appears he is perpetually preparing to whistle. Sometimes his teeth slip out, and when they do, he pulls his lip down like a window shade, tugging with his fingers.

By twilight we had done the roller coaster four times and the two of us were dizzy from all the loops and dips. We gorged ourselves on wieners. We visited the beer garden. We threw baseballs and made this girl in a striped bikini fall in a tank. George bought ten balls and dunked her every time but once. He said he liked the way she looked at him, just before he threw the ball. She had the flattest belly I have ever seen.

Everything glowed like Christmas. Everybody's boots made dust get in your nose. It was my birthday. We thought about taking a spin on the Ferris wheel but decided that would be queer. I bought myself a nice cotton candy. Then all that was left was the sideshow.

The barker was what you would expect—wearing an old top hot, a red coat with a forked tail, his mustache curled at the tips with earwax. He leaned against a podium, his chin in his hand. Surrounding him posters advertised many things including the world's smallest horse and the world's biggest hog, plus a savage beastman from the jungles of Tanzania, and so on.

Then there was my Bearded Lady.

Her picture was a crude rendering—very cartoonish, nothing to take note of, except her lips. The thought of them still makes me sweat, the vision of their pout and color, shining red, carefully lipsticked beneath her whiskers.

God!

When we walked up and slapped down our money, the barker's forehead got full of lines. I asked if he really had himself a bearded lady and he nodded and we squared our hats and went through the dusty flap.

The tent had a tremendous odor, somewhere between the hot stink of a noonday stall and the musk of a woman. It made my middle parts feel loose and warm and I took several bites from my cotton candy. It was so sweet as to make your teeth ache.

The horse was a pony and it was little, sure, but it was also standing in a hole. It hadn't been groomed, even brushed, probably ever. As for the hog—it wasn't spectacularly big by any means. "What's a hog need a chair for?" George said, referring to the small rocking chair in its cage, and I explained the illusion, the trick played on people like us.

The manbeast was a filthy ape suit crouched in a cage. I clawed up a hunk of sawdust and pegged its head and its head fell off to reveal straw guts.

Right then I lost my trust. Everything was phony—a *lie*—a waste of our time and quarters. Everything but The Bearded Lady. Such beauty as hers I had never before witnessed.

Yes, she later committed sordid indiscretions. Yes, there is a dead peanut of a child curled inside her dead belly—and, no, it is not of my get. I know this because we never performed such acts. It is not that I did not feel desire. I am ashamed to admit it is because my circulation is poor.

So poor my feet get cold and I wear wool socks, even come May.

She had needs. A woman of whiskers is a woman of passion and impulse. I harbor no blame. In spite of what happened, I still love her and I believe she loved me more than life, beard to bones.

They called it an aneurysm. It happened in the bathtub. It happened because of what she did, to me.

The first thing we saw was legs, crossed and moving like scissors, as if impatient or in need of urinary relief. Her calves were of the meat club variety. Some would call them man legs. She sat on a stool and wore a skirt, a short white one with a mess of red polka dots across it.

George and I were enraptured. He forgot about his teeth and they slipped out to gnaw his bottom lip. Even when he is drunk, this does not happen. I could hear the noises his tongue made. They were hungry noises.

We removed our hats in reverence.

Our eyes went up past her juicier regions, finally zeroing in on her beard. It was a full beard. It was blond and curly and she had woven daisies into its ringlets. That was a real sight. I correctly guessed she shampooed her whiskers on a regular schedule. Inside that nest of hairs were lips—pink and moist to point of obscenity.

What's worse: they gripped a cigarette.

I was driven mad by the sight! I wasn't sure if I wanted to crawl in my pocket or melt her down and take a sip.

What happened next is telling—*George* stepped forward. I would have, but instead took many wolfish bites from my cotton candy.

Since her death, I have revisited the past many a time. This is one moment I relate to the high danger and doublecrossings of what was to come. George took two steps, three, until he was abreast of the velvet rope that separated her from us. From the wild look in his eye, the urge to have relations seemed homicidal. It was that potent. I myself would have become big in the jeans if such a thing were possible. We both just wanted to fill her up, to fall into dreams of moist peace.

I now recognize those as shameful thoughts, considering how soft and genuine our love became.

I don't blame George.

She looked at him, did a wink thing, looked at me, released a cloud of smoke and said, "Hell-oo," in this nectarous voice.

George swallowed and his throat-apple slid around. He motioned at me with his thumb and said, "It's his birthday."

The Bearded Lady smiled a smile that made me feel like accomplishing touchdowns. She said, "Good for you, honey."

I pressed the cotton candy hard against my face, hard so that the paper cone dug into my lips. I could feel the fibrous sugar melting, sticking to my cheeks. I imagine now what I looked like then: me, with the apparition of a pink beard.

Perhaps it was this that kindled her original fancy?

Regardless, she chose me.

Courting a bearded lady is an arduous task. She is unpredictable. What I mean is she might flirt with someone on the street, in the bar, bat her eyelashes or lick her lips, just to see how you will react. I could not bear this and ended up in a handful of fistfights.

Which pleased her greatly.

Piece of advice: if courting a bearded lady, do not succumb to her persistent physical challenges. She is stronger than you. Never arm-wrestle or engage in foot races with her. You will lose.

Above all, a bearded lady is sensitive about her whiskers. I once made the mistake of recommending a trim. I don't think she ever forgave me. And I worshipped her beard, I *adored* it, but it was getting a little too ZZ Top for me. She wept for a whole day and when I said, "What can I do to make things better?" she said, "Stand still. Don't move. Close your eyes." I did as she said and she punched my lights out with a right cross to the temple.

I stopped trying to anticipate or understand.

When The Bearded Lady first visited my trailer at Lazy H, she was appalled at the conditions. "Won't do," she said, walking around with her hands folded behind her back like some sort of health food inspector. "Thought you were a better man than this," she said. "Smells like a barn," she said. She said if she fell asleep here she'd feel sorry about it in the morning.

I admit it's no Shan-Gri-La.

I showed her around the ranch, showed her Oregon's Organ. She referred to him as a mighty steed. I agreed and told her about his fluids, how we had shipped them as far as Texas. She asked how exactly we extracted these fluids. I told her that was George's gig—not mine—but if she absolutely had to know—and she did—you sprayed a sawhorse with hormones and from the sawhorse hung this big rubber oven-mitt thingy into which the horse stuck his doodad.

She said, "*You're* kidding?" in a voice you wouldn't use unless truly excited.

I said, "I am not."

We held hands some, and though she stepped in dung and complained about the black flies, I could tell she liked it here. Forget the carnival, another week and she had moved in for good.

To profess my love, I bought her things, things like dresses and fancy undergarments and expensive fruits from the grocery. We were together only five months, but she drained me dry.

Another thing I did, I tried to grow a beard. It was a miserable failure of a beard. This brought her great pleasure. She sat me down and counted all of my whiskers: thirty-three: mostly in the region of my upper lip. She said I was no better than a Chinaman. She heartily slapped me on the shoulder when she said, "Chinaman."

That afternoon—as if excited by my beardlessness—she forced me to attempt love acts several times. Nothing came of it.

She made me want to be virile, for her. For me, pillow talk was good enough.

Things got tense at Lazy H. Whenever The Bearded Lady sauntered by, twirling her sun umbrella, or brought me a Pepsi and a ham sandwich, you could practically smell George's frustration. His breath got all asthmatic and he started chucking hay bales around as if they had *insulted* him. He wanted her, is what it came down to—he wanted her bad.

I kept expecting him to want to talk about it or fight about it—but nope—he stayed silent and I minded my Ps and Qs, a little anxious, I admit, about the way he eyed me when handling a pitchfork.

We split up the chores. He spent a week breaking horses with these caballero Mexicans and I rotated the irrigation, I shoed up the bays, I brushed the golden coat of Oregon's Organ and collected his junk in a bowl to put through a sieve to put in a bottle to stick in the fridge, next to the Michelob, where it cooled into crisp lettucey cash.

George was pissed because A) She chose me, and B) I didn't visit the Wounded Soldier anymore. I felt bad in both respects and so one night proposed we all go out for a game of eight ball and a nice cold pitcher. He replied with a nod and a *yep*, and it was a brightly tuned *yep*, so I knew he looked forward to our little date.

He is not a bad dude.

The Wounded Soldier used to be a grange hall.

People still dance and go yip-yeehaw, but now the place is mainly a place of drinking. Way up in the rafters, bats hang and chirp and flutter their wings and their guano mixes with the spit and the beer polishing the floor.

We walked in like so: George and me and The Bearded Lady, The Bearded Lady wearing this pretty risky silk dress I bought her from the mail-order catalogue. It didn't get quiet or anything, like you'd expect, but there were many eyeballs trained in our direction, crawling all over her. I expected such. Of course there's the beard. Also, she was of ample bosom—and her cleavage was showcased in a way that made you blind.

Things started off fine. George and I are known and respected and friendly with most. A few horsemen with mustaches floated over to handshake and shoot the shit and we made introductions. They said it's a pleasure to meet you to The Bearded Lady and she said the like. We gathered up some mugs and a pitcher. We chalked our sticks and played a game.

George was in high spirits. He downed one whiskey and then another and chewed his way through the foam in his beer and even laughed a few times, showing off his teeth. When The Bearded Lady sank four stripes on the break, he shook his head and said, "What a woman!"

Her beard matched the color of the beer she downed in fast gulps. Her private hair was of the same shade.

A gang of men huddled near the pool table, intoxicated by her bending over, her handling of the stick. They spied from beneath the shadows of their broad white hats. They opened and closed their mouths in a lecherous way.

The Bearded Lady was perfectly aware of all this. Must have been just like back in her carnival heydays, all that staring. She liked it. I know this. She could have shot the nine-ball sure and clean, but chose a terrible angle instead. She *wanted* them to see. She bent over and raised up her rear in full display. What a rear she had.

Just like that, one of the cowboys floated in and grabbed her rear. He had a small pretty face. When she spun around and faced him, he just stood there and didn't know what to do.

From the look on her face, you would have thought she wanted to kiss him. Instead, she cocked her arm and swung with all her might and he went down, his mouth a great black O. Then she looked at me. Something both of cheer and expectancy bubbled in her eye. I have never been a violent man, but she made me into one. I used my boots on that pretty man's pretty face—and when I broke his nose it made a sound like the snap of a pistol's hammer—a sound that anticipates blood.

I hurt many men. I hurt them with fists, boots, elbows, *even* a broken bottle of beer—and my Bearded Lady loved me so much, you have no idea.

I told her the truth, but The Bearded Lady would not believe my circulation problems. She became really upset. She accused me of finding her the object of fright and disgust. I said, "Then why am I with you, for Christ's sake?" Weeping and strenuous physical battle ensued.

After we fought, as if it were a sort of sex, she smoked and we reconciled tangled in each other's arms, whispering affections. Her smoking always worried me on account of her whiskers. What if they were set aflame? It's corny as hell but her breath, puffs of tobacco against my face, reminded me of toast before getting mixed up with the powdery flavor of her perfume. I like toast a lot and when I went to kiss her, hungry for it, she shoved me away and said she didn't want somebody to kiss, she wanted somebody to sex her like an animal.

I said, "Jeez."

One time at the Wounded Soldier, I returned from the toilet only to discover George and The Bearded Lady holding hands. I watched from a short distance, hating them both with a strange affection. Then I coughed to announce my presence. George tried to pull his hand back, but she kept it firmly in her grasp. She was unashamed. She announced she was reading his palm. I pretended and wanted to believe this. She said George had a good soul and predicted a future of love and wealth and happiness.

Her predictions proved false.

Later that night she amazed us all by conquering the mechanical bull. This had never been done.

She whispered to me before falling into dreams. She whispered: goodnight, baby. I want to bottle this up and drink it. Whatever happened before didn't matter: she might have half-nelsoned me just fifteen minutes ago, she might have spit and clawed all over my body, burned my elbow with a cigarette: but when it was time for sleep, nothing mattered except those words. She said her mother—who was also a bearded lady by trade—taught her one thing and one thing only: never go to bed angry.

Had you been there, had you heard her sweet voice, I am certain you would love her also. I could not predict much about her behavior, but I knew this: every night, without exception, "Goodnight, baby."

Things became uncertain. What I do know is that she and George were lovers. I first became aware of this when I discovered a damp spot on the sheets. I put my nose to it and it smelled like mushrooms growing at the bottom of a well. It was man juice. Of that I am certain. What's worse, George admitted nothing. We went about our chores and he offered me so many smiles, perhaps trying to tooth away any suspicions.

The Bearded Lady was not satisfied with paints or bays, so I let her ride the tamer geldings in the holding pen. She would wear a sundress and smoke her cigarettes and grip the saddlehorn with her meaty hands and dig in her high heels like spurs and say, "Yaw! Yaw now!" Around and around she would go, the smoke streaming from her nostrils like tusks, her beard filling with dust. She said it reminded her of the carrousel.

Sometimes George and the Mexicans came and watched.

A horse can only get going so fast in a pen. "I want to gallop," she said. No, I said. "I want to ride Oregon's Organ." *No*, I said. She had a hankering for Oregon's Organ. It was a terrible hankering.

After an hour in the pen and she would go home and draw a cold bath. This was her antidote to the summer heat, not to mention her sexual frustrations. I would set up a rocking chair next to the tub and watch her, naked and beautiful, shampooing her beard, her nipples tightened into points, her bathing sounds sounding like a music I was unfamiliar with.

She would say, "Dear, dear, dear," pressing me to the walls and floors, her beard tickling my cheeks. She would say, "Goodnight, baby," when we stared at each other across the pillows. I was cow-eyed with love.

One minute things were great—the next, not so much.

She would go bananas, wearing me out, hollering about how she didn't have a thing—not one *thing*—to wear. Hollering about how she wanted to ride old Oregon's Organ, about how I didn't respect and satisfy her *needs* as a lady. When we quarreled, it was usually me saying how sorry I was without knowing why.

Then I caught her surrendering to George.

I walked in and there they were. She was splayed out over the couch with her rear up in the air. He was really going to town on it and she offered him plenty of verbal encouragement. I stood there a while and observed their joined condition. George brought his teeth down and raked them across her back as if her back was the cream center of an Oreo cookie.

I had seen enough. I slammed the door behind me and they stopped but didn't even look at me, didn't even separate, but laid there, tangled and breathing heavily and trying to figure out what to do, what to say.

What happened next I would never have guessed. George came after me. He was naked save for a pair of white tube-socks. His gonad stood at attention. I thought he would stab me with it. I dodged him and brought my fist to his mouth. His teeth cut me to the bone. I still bear scars.

I believe he meant to kill me.

Again he charged, scepter at the fore. Fighting a naked man is not difficult. This time I tripped him. He fell upon himself. There was a sound not unlike the snap of a bite of celery. I will not go into the details, but know this: George will never be the same man.

She looked at me. It was a look of terrific shame. Her mouth opened with what was probably an apology. I lifted my hand like a cigar-store Indian. Only my hand wasn't saying *hello*. My hand was saying *be quiet*. My hand was saying something about hate. She understood this. Her beard shivered when she closed her mouth. Here was her most vulnerable moment.

I didn't stick around. I stepped over moaning George and went straight to the Wounded Soldier and drank my way into a terrible drunk. Sometime that night The Bearded Lady drew a cold bath, and died. The water got her heart rate up, something burst at the top of her neck. Her brain drowned above water. She died in and out of love.

The mortician did something awful. First, he goes and tells me The Bearded Lady was four weeks with child. Second, he shaves off her beard. Says it will make her more presentable for the funeral.

Staring at her freshly shaven, freshly makeupped corpse, I felt little in the way of emotion. I looked at her clean upper lip, her cheeks of pink stone, and felt nothing. Because *this* was not The Bearded Lady. It was the beard that made her *such* a woman. It was the beard that made her both fragile and venomous, somehow.

Strange as it sounds, this woman laid out cold before me looked more than ever like a man. A man who knew how to chop firewood and chug a beer and cook a quality steak. Except for that lipstick, except for those magnificent breasts, I might have bought this man a beer and shook his hand.

I didn't want a thing to do with a funeral. No wake. No words. No next of kin. Just close up the casket and nail it tight and for crying out loud put *her* in the ground.

I keep a still life in the living room. On the coffee table there is a *Cosmopolitan* magazine and an old apple—dried-up and wrinkled like some animal's heart—and an ashtray full of lipstick-stained cigarettes. All this helps me imagine she is just in the other room, maybe visiting the toilet, maybe still soaking in a cold bath.

I know George is a good man. I can't blame him. He has suffered duly. We still drink at Wounded Soldier, work at Lazy H, though there is an awkwardness between us, and he spends most of his time with the Mexicans. He claims he is more suited for stable and fieldwork these days.

I have taken over all duties involving Oregon's Organ.

Oregon's Organ is getting famous by the minute. This August he was named West Coast Reserve Champion. The promise of his get makes most salivate—his golden color, the beauty of his architecture. He is a grand machine. We breed him like crazy.

Practically every day he goes to work on one of the local mares or else a fluid shipment heads off for Texas or Montana. He is the busiest stallion. I suspect he is happy. I take him out sometimes and his hooves divot the pasture and we ride so hard and long that my eyes burn from the wind and my body trembles with gratitude. He does exactly what he is told and my tame control of this power beneath me is wonderful and exotic thing.

I think I know how she felt.

I think I am beginning to know what it means to wear a beard.

Swans

Weekends, Drew bicycled to Huntington Lake, where the Aloha cheerleaders gathered to sunbathe and swim and dive off the high granite cliffs. He liked watching them, when they didn't know they were being watched, at the sandy cove where they spread their neon beach towels and oiled their bodies and drank rum and Pepsi.

Nobody knew about the cove, really—not about the deer that drank from it, dampening their hooves, nor the crawdads that slept in its beds of warm mud, nor the many panfish shining beneath its water like precious stones—nobody except Drew, his friend Kenny, and the cheerleaders.

Nobody knew about it because a storm brought some logs down the Harpeth River and into the lake where they settled at the mouth of the cove, camouflaging it, and Drew, making a nice shady spot for the brown trout and the Coho salmon to doze.

Here he floated, among the logs and the slippery creatures, his eyes just above the surface, like an alligator, watching so long his skin got wrinkled and the fish considered him just another part of the lake, something to nuzzle and chew, to rub with their scales, and occasionally, when they wrapped their sharp sucking mouths around his feet and tasted them, he wanted to move but didn't. He rarely moved—not even when the powerboats ripped by and shifted the logs and disturbed the garter snakes nesting there—and he never made a sound, never moaned, never screamed I-love-yous at the girls.

Though he wanted to.

He loved them with everything he had. He loved them more than anything in the world. The water was warm and he floated there, pretending the girls belonged to him, like dolls, and if he wanted to kiss them or hold them or anything else—anything at all—they would gladly succumb to it.

Sometimes Drew brought along his friend Kenny. Kenny was tiny and fine-boned and got thrown in garbage cans a lot. He could swallow an entire banana and bring it back up. It was spooky. He liked the cheerleaders, too, but feared the snakes and the dragonflies and Drew always worried he might suffer a screaming attack and ruin everything.

Sometimes—bobbing in the water, algae clinging to his bald cheeks—Kenny whispered all the unbelievable things he wanted to do to the cheerleaders, his voice accelerating into a quivery pressure-cooker hiss that bothered Drew.

It made him feel grotesque. Like he had been caught doing something embarrassing. It made him feel fat and fifteen, which he was, with hair only beginning to bud in his armpits.

You keep quiet and listen to your fantasies—Drew thought—and it sounds like God is talking to you. You say them out loud, you expose them to the air, and you *ruin* them, as it is with copper.

Drew preferred the sound of the frogs drumming,

the lakewater softly popping against the logs, the girls laughing. He preferred to forget who he was, even where he was, his eyes tearing from the sunlight on the water, making everything glittery, like the best kind of dreams, where you are never afraid and everything turns out for the best.

Around noon, when the sun burned away all the clouds, when the air just trembled with humidity—making the girls look like some mirage you prayed was real—they ate their tiny lunches of baby carrots and yogurt and tortilla chips before climbing the nearby hill, through the hardwood forest, and assembling at the jumping place, the granite cornice that jutted above the water, maybe fifty feet above it.

There was never any wind—Drew could hear everything they said—which was how he learned her name was Jessica.

She was the most beautiful among them—her hair as brown as her belly, as brown as a bean—and maybe her beauty gave her bravery, because she always jumped first—her legs tight together, her feet pointed down—screaming ya-ya-ya until the lake swallowed her with a *ploosh*.

A bubbling curl of water lingered where she broke it.

This was Drew's favorite part, when he adjusted his goggles and took big gulps of air and dove down among the salmon and trout, flapping his arms, palms up, so that he might remain submerged long enough to see her bikini torn away when she struck the lake, revealing her breasts, so pale against her brown body, surrounded by the grayish green nowhere of underwater.

Never was anything so beautiful as she was then, her hair swirl-ing, her bikini twisted around her neck, her eyes closed, her mouth open in an oval, savoring the casual danger of the jump, the elastic acceptance of the water.

She made you want to cry, just seeing her.

When she scissored her legs—so smooth and innocent to all the evil things that lurked beneath—when she kicked her way to the surface, the water rippled and bubbled, the bubbles rolling off her skin to form a shiny ribbon, twisting in her wake, soon vanishing.

Drew wondered what the water felt like to Jessica—and what it would feel like to be the water, cleaning her, embracing her, finding his way into her every crevice.

Here is what it would feel like to seep between her legs—he decided—it would feel like the lake mud feels when it swallows your foot to the ankle, a warm obliging pull.

Drew lived in Overall. Overall is just outside Aloha.

Everybody who lived in Overall wished they lived in Aloha and everybody who lived in Aloha knew this and reveled in it.

Here, in Overall, five stoplights swayed over the wide empty streets. Here, in blocky black and red letters, billboards advertised Budweiser, Marlboro, and Lynyrd Skynyrd playing at the Rutherford County Fair.

Here a dusty Dairy Queen sign read, "OVERALL. WE LIKE WHO WE ARE."

Here a deer crossed the highway and hurdled a barbed-wire fence, rolls of alfalfa moldered in the fields, a farmer chased palomino horses with his pickup. Here was the Feed and Seed, the First Baptist Church, the Piggly Wiggly, the Pinch Penny Tavern, the Old Hickory Trailer Park, hidden among the pines, where the shadows gathered in bluer shades, as if trapped deep underwater.

That was Overall.

A rifle shot's distance and you were past it, you were going to Aloha, where they had a Cineplex and a Wal-Mart Supercenter and beautiful cheerleaders who did high kicks and somersaults and flashed their clean white panties, where—as Drew saw it—life seemed a better thing.

Every Friday night was the same old story.

Around eight o'clock, when the bats and the owls and a deep purplish color rose from the forest and filled the sky, the Aloha footballers paid Overall a visit. Everyone gathered on the sidewalks and on their lawns, in lawn chairs, as you would for a parade, with cold cans of Bud Light tucked into Amoco cozies, with bags of jerky balanced on their thighs, waiting for the footballers to come.

And then they came.

Their tricked-out Cameros and El Caminos and cherry-red Chevy pickups made a collective noise that started as a barely perceptible whine—you could hear it a long way off—and rose to a grumbling shout that rolled into Overall like a deeply gray thunderhead.

Probably they went a hundred-miles-per-hour—that was what people said—but who could know for sure.

They were so fast, they were their own kind of fast. Their speed was such that it ruffled Drew's hair and popped his ears. Their speed made him jealous, like: I wish I had the guts. They tore through the streets and parking lots and slammed their brakes and cranked their steering wheels so hard they spun around corners, tires smoking, blistering, melting, leaving behind swirling rubber designs for Overall to remember them by, until next Friday.

Of course the cops chased them.

Overall had two cops whose singular duty, it seemed, was to chase the footballers while everyone watched, not cheering like maybe you'd expect, just watching, for the spectacle, knowing the cops didn't really want to catch anybody, and even if they did, they would never be fast or brave enough.

The footballers hurled eggs and crumpled beer cans, they tooted their horns, they did donuts in the park and screamed mostly unintelligible screams about your mother, before zooming back to Aloha and leaving Drew, trembling, slightly dizzy, with their noise still in his head.

They had done this for years. It was their custom, as it was Overall's to watch, afraid and panicked and excited at once, not really understanding why they sat around and let the footballers beat them, only knowing it was horribly entertaining, somehow.

Drew's father, Marty, called himself the fish czar. Which sounded a lot better than Washington County's senior fisheries biologist. He spent his days in waders, catching steelhead and king salmon and sturgeon and measuring and tagging them, collecting scales, classifying and reclassifying rivers on their ability to support good salmon habitat, that kind of thing.

Sometimes he gutted fish and examined their spiralized guts and made marks in his little black notebook. Sometimes he gathered their eggs, as crisp and yellow as corn kernels, to look at under a microscope.

And sometimes he caught fish
so big they scared him.

The man had energy. Of that Drew was certain. Forever clapping his hands and smiling and jumping from the sofa to answer the phone with a *yello*. No matter how early, when Drew woke in the morning, there his father was, at the kitchen table, spreading marmalade across wheat toast, never drinking coffee or Coca-Cola, claiming he didn't need it, apparently drawing his energy from a source deep inside, some warm mineral spring of a source that Drew often wished he could bottle and drink.

Though Drew sometimes wondered, was that an all-over smile, when his father showered so long the house filled with steam, when late at night wet choking sounds fluttered down the hall, seeping through the crack under the door to wake Drew.

Marty handled so many fish, their smell crept into his skin and followed him around and stayed behind to introduce him. It was a sharp oily smell, something you might find at the bottom of a well. Drew didn't mind it except when the kids at school said he smelled not good, as in funny, *spermy*.

The two of them didn't have much to talk about—

"That was great," Drew would say when they finished a movie or a meal, and Marty would say, "Wasn't it?"—but they loved each other. They loved each other a lot, in the unsaid brutish way that fathers and sons acknowledge such a thing, with slugs to the shoulder, wrestling matches.

Fishing away their afternoons on a skiff.

When they fished, they wrapped peanut butter balls around their hooks and plopped them in the water and hung bells from their lines, so that they might nap, together, with their caps pulled low, sometimes so startled by the bell's ringing they screamed and grabbed each other.

Then they reeled in what was oftentimes a rainbow trout, sometimes a walleye, and removed the hook and tossed the fish back in the water because they didn't enjoy killing. It wasn't in their hearts. Both of them were tender in this way—a certain combination of bruised and gentle—no thanks to *her*.

She left them to marry Shane Harvey, a.k.a. Donut, the former Overall High defensive coach, whose early retirement led to an offensively lopsided football team led to a series of chronic and devastating losses led to the Friday night troubles with Aloha.

She and Donut moved north, to Washington, where the air tasted like a cold drink of water, people claimed.

Washington was a place Drew never wanted to go.

Sometimes he forgot what she looked like. Like everyday her memory sank deeper inside, where it was slowly digested, broken down into little particles that cried their way out of him late at night when he buried his face in his pillow. And soon there would be nothing left? How could he resent what he couldn't remember? Sometimes he wanted to chew grass like a sick dog and throw her back up.

And sometimes he dug through the closet and wiped the dust from the wedding album and saw her and his father, happy and hopeful and running down the aisle.

"That bitch," Drew wanted to say, "that fucking bitch!" Though he kept quiet, keeping his anger for his mother as he kept his love for the cheerleaders, nested inside him, like a seed.

Drew went down, beneath the water lilies and logs, past the trout that nipped playfully at his shorts and toes—five, ten, twenty feet—until he reached the lake's muddy bottom, until the blood pulsing in his head matched that in his groin.

Down was a good place to be.

Below him were bird and fish bones tangled in the roots of silky grasses. Above him were the black silhouettes of trout, lazily whipping their tails back and forth, and beyond them, a rippling sky, colored white and orange and blue, like an enormous church window forever reorganizing itself into little crescents and diamonds, sparkling.

There was nothing else. There was nothing to say and nothing to hear—no powerboats, no airplanes, no frogs, no Kenny whispering his hunger for the cheerleaders—nothing to do except resist the alternate gravity that took hold of his fat and tugged upward.

He embraced a slimy boulder and held tight. Here his mind was single. Here he plugged into his pulse and yielded to it. A rainbow trout brushed past him, its scales the brightest thing in the water until the girls crashed through the ceiling of the lake, every one of them beautiful, with their breasts bared and their arms wide open.

He could hold his breath a long time—he practiced at home and at school, sometimes gasping in the back row and making everyone turn around and laugh—and so he waited for Jessica. Even when black and red spots danced across his retinal screen, he waited.

When she finally appeared above him, surrounded by a white column of bubbles, as if she were boiling hot, the blood came rushing to his face and bordered on causing an aneurysm, struck as he was by the misery that was his desire. Earlier that day he found himself suddenly aroused and in a pinch ended up jerking off not into his own hand or sock—that would be pathetic enough—but into his mother's bedroom slipper, the one shaped like a bear claw, which she left behind and which they had not bothered to throw away.

Now, among the black leeches and crawdads, he felt the impulse to grab her ankles and drag her down, swallow her with his arms, *squeeze*, until they both lost their breath and perished, thrilled and doomed.

But together.

And this was April, when the swans came.

The Aloha footballers—who played baseball now but who fundamentally remained footballers, swinging at every pitch, swinging with everything they had, sometimes forgetting to drop the bat and charging first base with it tucked in the crook of their arm, other times tackling a runner to make certain he was *out*—they won their sixth straight game and the cheerleaders celebrated this by drinking their way deep into a rum drunk.

At the cove they skipped stones and practiced their cheers and their human pyramid and when it collapsed they laughed so hard they cried, their nearly naked bodies tangled together in the sand. Then, after they sunbathed and ate some lunch and jumped off the cliffs, forwards, backwards, hand-in-hand, Jessica pulled a hatchet from her backpack and announced they would build a raft.

It was a hot day full of flies that tasted their sweat when they took turns with the hatchet, in their bikinis. There was just enough fat on their bodies so that when they swung, when they chopped at the dogwood trees, they jiggled. It was erotic, somehow. They put their hair in ponytails and wiped their faces with their forearms and bound the logs with rope, the sap sticking to their skin, the sand sticking to the sap, and together they dragged the raft to the lake. When they discovered it floated, kind of, they celebrated with more rum and collapsed on their towels and fell asleep.

Drew and Kenny watched all this all day and into the early evening, their chins and cheeks glistening from where the water touched them, their hands pale and wrinkled with strange hieroglyphic designs.

If you could read the designs they might say something about being alone and being in love.

Owls called. Bats swooped down and seized mayflies and moths off the logs, making Kenny nervous. He said, "Maybe we should go," and Drew didn't say anything but shook his head, *no*. The sun eased toward the horizon, into the forest, setting the white oak and blue ash and dogwood aflame, their tops haloed with a light red light that slowly darkened to clay's redness.

Out of this came the swans.

There were about twenty of them altogether, all flapping and honking and making a very big noise when they circled the lake, flying together but not like geese do, a tangled white cloud that descended on the cove, their wings breezing silvery ripples on the water when they slowed and settled there.

The cheerleaders woke up and made high sounds of appreciation when they raced down the beach and into the lake. Here they laughed and tasted rum from their Styrofoam cups and said, "Pretty," and "Would you look at that? Would you just *look* at that?" and "Can you believe those are swans. I mean, *swans*, for Christ's sake."

They waded until the water came to their thighs, a short distance from the swans, approaching the flock as they approached the jumping place, with Jessica leading them, unafraid, innocent to the awfulness of nature.

The sunset flared and for a moment you could see every shadow and broken feature of the land, and the swans seemed to glow a phosphorescent white, white like you wouldn't believe.

They were fat—off cattails and duckweed and water moss—and they wanted to get fatter. They were hungry. Drew wondered where they had been and what they had seen that made them so hungry when they dunked their heads in the water, searching for something to eat. One swan withdrew a crawdad and chewed it until it cracked, pleasuring in its soft gray muscle and sour green guts.

The air darkened to a purplish color and as if on cue the swans moved toward the girls without appearing to move, gliding, like ghosts, with little collars of foam trailing behind them. The girls watched them come, with their arms wrapped casually around each other's waists and shoulders, with Jessica asking, "Do we got any bread? I bet they want bread."

Then the swans opened their six-foot wingspans and lowered their heads and straightened their necks and a tremendous hiss filled the air, a noise associated with snakes and flat tires, with imminent danger, a noise that told the girls to run.

So they ran. They splashed their way to shore and ran along the beach, squealing with frightened pleasure, the sand sticking to their feet. And the swans followed. Their great white shapes lifted from the water as if drawn by invisible wires, gracefully, effortlessly, honking and hissing and striking the girls with the big blocks of air that came rolling out from under their wings.

Drew wanted to help. But it was easier to watch.

Some of the girls screamed, others tripped in their drunkenness and scrambled forward on all fours and began to cry in panicky gulps when claws raked red lines across their butts and backs. They abandoned their towels and coolers and crashed off into the brushwood where they could be heard for a long time, wailing like sirens, branches snapping, leaves sizzling beneath their bare feet so you would have thought the whole forest was pulling up its skirt to dance.

Kenny said, "Cool."
Drew said, "I'm worried about this."

The next weekend Drew and Kenny visited the cove and found the swans there, roosting on the beach and on the raft, bobbing in the water, coiling their necks—necks as long and slender as a woman's arm—into positions that made you question the existence of the bone within them.

The boys entered the cove from the small lakeside inlet, plunging deep before swimming forward, to avoid the giant garter snakes that gathered in nests that looked like twisting balls. Once underwater Drew heard that sound—the one everyone heard—the pulsing of a heart, but when he surfaced it was gone.

Where are they? he wondered. Where is *she*?

He pictured a town, Aloha, a house, hers. Probably she lived in the same kind of house everyone lived in around here, ranch-style with a brick exterior, with white gutters and white trim surrounding the windows and doors. Probably she just stepped from the shower, he thought, and now stood opposite the bathroom mirror, combing her hair with a horsehair brush, her breasts flattened by the neon towel wrapped around her body. Surely she thought about the lake, the jumping place, the rush of wind when the water rose to meet her. Surely she would come.

He felt a pounding in his chest and in his groin. He tried to calm it, imagining it as aligned with the breaking of the water against the logs, a vision ruined by an enormous trout slipping its mouth around his foot, a moistly violent sensation just obscene enough to stroke him all over.

When Kenny said, “Maybe they aren’t—” Drew put a finger to his lips that told him to be quiet.

Finally she came, along with the rest, but only to retrieve their towels and coolers, which the swans had ravaged and shit upon, thoroughly.

The girls stood where the beach met the trees, shading their eyes, watching the swans nap with their heads tucked under their wings, and from a distance—with their scooped backs—the swans looked like tremendous molars and the lake looked like a lake full of teeth.

Whereas the other girls darted forward and snatched their things and hurried back to the safety of the trees, Jessica sauntered out and stood with her legs apart and yelled, “Hey!” The swans paid her no attention. “Hey, fuckers,” she said and picked up a rock and hurled it at a nearby swan, striking its back. The swan released a surprised honk before uncurling its neck and sighting Jessica and departing the water with one determined snap of its wings.

She had wild happy look on her face when she lifted her hands to accept its body and together they crashed to the sand.

She fought in a way that reminded Drew of dancing—swirling, crouching, leaping, sometimes closing her eyes when she found a steady rhythm—and she did this as she did everything, with abandon. There was no turning back—and so even if she bled, even if she fell in a tangle now and then, she would right herself, she would lean forward at the waist and move her arms and legs and continue to fight.

The swans gathered on one side, the cheerleaders on the other, each voicing their encouragement with honks, screams, each scurrying forward and then back, as if eager and afraid to join the violence.

A perspective Drew understood completely when he swam from his hiding place and dashed along the beach and joined the girls—who paid him no attention—soon followed by Kenny.

Her lip curled back in a snarl, her muscles jumped beneath her skin, her hands needed no instruction, knowing what to do, where to go, a left hook to the wing, a chop to the neck, even as the swan snapped its beak, pinching her chest and arms, hissing.

It was a beautiful thing to watch.

Then, in exhaustion, she wrapped her arms around the swan and the swan curled its neck around hers, so that they seemed but one fantastic creature that eventually broke apart—and when she and the swan retreated to the woods and to the lake, each of them breathing in asthmatic bursts that revealed how badly they hurt, Drew imagined approaching Jessica.

The girls would part before him, zipper-style, and there she would be, bleeding and hurting but putting on a big show, giving him the thumbs-up when he asked was she okay, did she need anything, *any*thing at all? "No," she would say, "nothing," and he would brush from her face a damp strand of hair and she would close her eyes a moment, savoring his touch, still panting from the fight, looking both fierce and vulnerable. "You're worried about me," she would say. "That's sweet." And then they would bring their mouths together, hard, making blood. Hers would be sweet, like maraschino cherries, and the cheerleaders would murmur all around them.

I should totally do that, Drew thought. I should kiss her and carry her home. That would be brave. That's what I'm going to do *right now*.

But he didn't—and the girls disappeared between the trees, touching Jessica and following her to where the clay game-trail turned to the gravel path turned to the asphalt road that led to the highway, and after that, Aloha.

Friday night came and so did the footballers. They entered Overall en masse—ten Camaros, three pickups, and a salmon-colored El Camino, all with their mufflers drilled to make their noise bigger, all with faces leering and hollering through their open windows—and then they split apart, some of them blazing along the main strip, others diving down side streets.

From all corners of the town they squealed their tires and honked their horns, like birds answering each other. Police sirens joined their noise and the effect was strangely musical, not something you could tap your foot to, but nice.

Drew watched all this from the sidewalk, along with his father and Kenny and the rest of Overall, watching like you would watch a sporting event, jealous of and awed by the players' upsetting power. He drank from a glass bottle of root beer that sweated in his hand. He kept the bottle to his lips when a Camaro came tearing by, its wheels rising on one side when it took the corner, followed by a cop car.

Marty was being Marty. He was being happy. Except to say *duck*, he ignored the beer cans thrown in their direction. Instead he pointed out the footballers when they zoomed past, saying *hey*, that's so-and-so, who broke the Washington County rushing record.

Like everyone else he paid careful attention to Aloha, subscribing to their newspaper, *The Mondo Times*, sometimes reading it twice in one sitting, holding it close to his face, studying names and scores and obituaries, as if they were the most important things.

"Man," he said, his voice a joyful shout you would not use unless imitating joy. "Holy smokes, did you see that? He drives as fast as he runs."

A couple Boy Scouts walked by selling popcorn and Marty bought a bag off them. He passed it to Drew and said, "Isn't this great, guys? Drew?"

Drew didn't say anything. For some reason he felt bothered by his father, the way he clapped his hands, the way he smiled so big the corners of his mouth twitched slightly. He saw him as if for the first time, and it was like something thrown at you when you weren't looking. It was annoying and it was shocking. His father's face remained an old familiar happy thing but beneath it he seemed sick.

Drew could smell the fish smell puffing off his father and though it had never bothered him, it bothered him now as a smell that partnered a fever, a bad one, one that keeps you up all night, sweating.

He tried concentrating on his popcorn, which made him thirsty, so he guzzled his root beer down, only to spit a mouthful out his nose, hacking for breath when one of the pickups rocketed past with a blonde cheerleader hanging out its window, giving him the finger, her face painted blue, orange and white, *their* colors. From the open bed three more girls—*his* girls—shook their pom-poms and cheered, "Aloha!" while the wind knocked their hair every which way.

"Oh, great," Kenny said. "Now they're in on it, too." He lifted his thin arms and let them fall. "Wonderful."

Marty said, "Pretty sure that was Hank Haines. Heck of a quarterback, that guy."

Drew now studied the window of every passing car. He sought her face and hoped he would not find it. He hoped she was better than this. He drank more root beer and his throat moved up and down as if something was trapped there.

Then the El Camino fishtailed around the corner and came to a sliding stop, and though Drew didn't recognize her at first—with her face painted blue on one side, white on the other—this was her, this was Jessica, the girl he wanted to know in so many ways. She sat on the passenger side, the side facing him, and he wondered was she *with* the dumb ape behind the steering wheel? He hoped not.

She looked at Drew and he liked being looked at. *She sees me*! he thought. *We are having a moment*. He interpreted the moment as one exchanged between two strangers who meet unexpectedly, in the forest, at the mall, and develop in one lingering glance that weird kind of closeness people get when they know zero about each other but *feel* a deep connection. Then she smiled at he didn't know what, and he wondered what she saw, a fat boy or something else.

He raised a hand to her: she copied the gesture.

And an egg, launched from her hand, struck his face, oozing into his eyes and mouth. With equal effect she might have punched him in the guts. He felt all the hope knocked black from his body—though the longing was still there.

She laughed, her mouth wide open and holding a shadow, and the El Camino took off and she was gone, so elusive, yet lingering, like the pain that wakes you from a dream and ends up belonging to the dream.

Kenny laughed, too, before choking it back, knowing better but still smiling.

Drew didn't bother wiping away the egg. Instead he held his head in his hands as if it were something separate from him. He could hear the anger mounting in his breathing.

Marty said, "Are you okay? Are you okay?" He looked emotional enough to kiss Drew on the mouth. To prevent this from happening Drew took another root beer from the cooler and drank it in one long gurgling swallow that foamed a belch up his throat that took longer to get out than the root beer took to get in. He kept the bottle against his lips and when his father asked again, was he okay, he said, "I'm fine."

The words dropped in the bottle and broke.

Sometimes—not very often but *some*times—when Drew and Marty were out on the skiff, sucking the peanut butter off their thumbs and waiting for the bells to ring, they talked. Marty would talk about the nurse shark he landed at Beverly Beach, Oregon, how it took him an entire afternoon, and how the shark kept biting at the air, at nothing, long after it died. He would talk about the Labrador puppy he once found inside a sturgeon's stomach, whole, with its tiny pink tongue stuck out. And he would talk about women. The girls he dated in high school and in college. But never—not ever—did he talk about *her*.

At times like these Drew felt more like a friend than a son of any sort, his father seeming at once younger than him and like an old man who remembered life sweeter than it honestly was.

So Marty talked and Drew listened and they laughed when zipping up and down Washington County's lakes and reservoirs and along the streams that sometimes petered out into salty marshes crowded with mosquitoes and turtles and mossy trees, the middle of nowhere.

Marty knew where to find the fish. Sometimes they would be where two rivers converged, feeding in the eddies, hungry for the swirling larvae. Other times they would be where the willows hung off the banks or where the logs piled up, hiding in the shade, which seemed to Drew a good place to go. Where the fish were depended on the time of day, the time of year, but Marty knew where to find them.

On one of these trips he showed Drew the most amazing thing.

At the time he was working on a study that estimated the walleye's annual growth and reproduction cycles. For this he used a mini-boom shocker, a small device with a generator the size of a microwave and a rod he lowered from the skiff into the water, applying 400 volts that first drew toward the anode every fish within a hundred feet, and then, with a simple twist of the output settings, effectively paralyzed them, so that the surface of the water suddenly filled with convulsing fish you could pluck from the water with your hands.

Drew noticed how Marty smiled the whole time. He always smiled, sure, but right then, when the fish rose and tremored and gaped in pain, he looked *truly* happy. He looked like the footballers looked when they terrorized Overall, like Jessica looked when she dove off the cliffs, like his mother looked when she walked out the door with a suitcase in each hand. He looked like he felt good.

Drew knew what he needed to do. When his father showered and the house filled with steam, he stole from the skiff the mini-boom shocker and with bungee cords strapped it between the handlebars of his bicycle.

It was noon and it was hot when he arrived at the cove. The swans napped with their heads tucked away. Flies buzzed around them. The raft had run aground and he carried the shocker there. The logs were slick with guano. With not a little effort he shoved off the raft and climbed halfway onto it, legs kicking, propelling him toward where the swans waited, now awake and yawning and stretching like people.

Near the middle of the cove he crawled all the way onto the raft and held his breath when the swans inched toward him, fanning out to surround the raft, shifting nervously, cocking their heads, opening and closing their wings to pound the water. One of them showed its sharp pink tongue and hissed and the hissing quickly spread among the other swans, so loud and terrifying that it became the only thing.

For a second Drew didn't know what to do—hugging himself, he felt lost—but only for a second. He reached for the rod and lowered it into the water and knobbed on the power to 400 volts, like his father showed him.

Their hisses transformed to shrieks. It was a sound Drew never imagined he might cause—it sounded like women in pain or in sexual climax—but he did not stop and neither did they—they continued to move toward him—and so he upped the voltage.

Beneath their screams was an *under*sound, the sound of the mini-boom, an angry buzzing as electric currents crackled into the water, currents whose yellow fingers snapped and popped and took hold of the perch and the trout and the eels and leeches and drew them to the raft so that the water gradually darkened and stirred with their presence.

So many creatures broke the surface, seizuring, rolling over and over, showing their pale bellies, that the cove just shook, just boiled. The swans crawled more than swam toward the raft. The smell of fish was everywhere. Next to the raft a steelhead rose, its muddy eyes rolling back in its head, its sharp ugly face gaping in silent agony, and then, as if its pain belonged to him, Drew began to weep in the open way men normally avoid. He couldn't help it. He cried as he had never cried before. He cried over everything and nothing.

Never had he felt so powerful and repulsive and so awfully *good.*

The swans were nearly upon him when he switched the output settings from an alternating current to a direct current—a switch that caused muscle paralysis and illuminated the water with flashes of light—and the buzzing sound vanished, replaced a heavy arterial pulsing that Drew recognized.

The swans went quiet and limp, their necks collapsing, their wings unfolding, so that they just floated there, among the fish, not dead, but not wholly alive. Still sobbing, Drew switched off the mini-boom and picked them from the water, stacking their trembling bodies on the raft to put elsewhere so that the girls might return to him, falling from the sky with their arms wide open, their faces beautiful.

Acknowledgements

Thanks, first and foremost, to my parents, Peter and Susan, who gave me everything. Thanks to my sister, Jen. To Carolyn Fairfield, to Dave and Cynthia Moore, for their encouragement. And thanks to my beloved grandfather and grandmother, Harry and Louise Percy, for their wisdom and love and grace.

I am indebted to Mike Magnuson—buddy, teacher, Viking—who taught me how to put a sentence together, just as I owe the world to the venerable Brady Udall, whose stories remind me why I write stories.

A grateful nod to the lovely and brilliant Katherine Fausset. Much love to my favorite gang of uglies: Dan "Mexico" Levine, Matt "Old Man" Santiago, Amant "Big J" Dewan, and Michael "The Gerbil" Weisberg. Bear hugs and kidney punches to my Murfreesboro crew—Dean Bakopoulos, Jeremy Chamberlin, Holiday Reinhorn, Lisa Lerner, and Kathleen Hughes—who know exactly what I mean when I say, "Heaven is pals." Thanks to CJ Hribal and my colleagues at Marquette. Thanks to Robin Russell and Howard Saver, for the laughs and drinks and fellowship. Thanks to Elm Street. Thanks to Craig Bodoh and Mark Ranum, to Jake and Julia Stratman, to Tabare Alvarez, Scott Beem, Clint Cargile, Gillian King, and all my Carbondale cronies. To Allison Joseph, Jon Tribble, Beth Lordan, Rodney Jones. To Charles Fanning, for sending me to Ireland. Thanks, thanks, thanks.

Thanks to Sharon Dilworth for lighting the way. To all the literary journals who have published my work, but in particular to Jim Clark and Brandon Rauch at Greensboro, to Mitch Wieland and Patti Knox at Idaho, to Kyle Minor at FrostProof—thanks for believing in me.

To the good folks at Sewanee—Wyatt Prunty and Cheri Peters—my warmest thanks for two weeks of heaven and gin. Bless you for that. To Tony Earley and Janet Peery. To Elwood Reid. To Bobby Arellano and Meredith Steinbach. I'm grateful to Dave and Lynn and all the rest of the Dummer and Spielman clan for their support and friendship. And to Dan Wickett—for his generosity and for his undying and selfless commitment to literary fiction. Everyone, immediately, get online and join his Emerging Writers' Network. Now.

And for her constant faith, love, goofiness, and friendship, this book is dedicated to my wife, Lisa.

Carnegie Mellon University Press
Series in Short Fiction

Fortune Telling
David Lynn

A New and Glorious Life
Michelle Herman

The Long and Short of It
Pamela Painter

The Secret Names of Women
Lynne Barrett

The Law of Return
Maxine Rodburg

The Drowning and Other Stories
Edward Delaney

My One and Only Bomb Shelter
John Smolens

Very Much Like Desire
Diane Lefer

A Chapter From Her Upbringing
Ivy Goodman

Happy or Otherwise
Diana Joseph

Narrow Beams
Kate Myers Hanson

Now You Love Me
Liesel Litzenburger

The Genius of Hunger
Diane Goodman

The Demon of Longing
Gail Gilliland

Lily in the Desert
Annie Dawid

Slow Monkeys and Other Stories
Jim Nichols

Ride
David Walton

Wrestling With Gabriel
David Lynn

Inventing Victor
Jennifer Bannan

How to Fly
Rachael Perry

The Smallest People Alive
Keith Banner